Obsidian Heart

Obsidian Heart

BY

TRACY WILSON

http://beautifulpublications.com

Published by
Beautiful Publications LLC
Stratford, CT 06614

This book is a work of fiction. Names, characters, places, and incidents are either products of the author's imagination or are used fictitiously. Any resemblance to actual events or locales or persons, living or dead, is entirely coincidental.

PRINT ISBN: 978-1-7356620-7-7
EBOOK ISBN: 978-1-7356620-6-0

Printed in the United States of America

Introduction

I've been interested in 'New Age' for many years. I didn't talk about it too much when I was younger because I was often told I was weird. It was safe when my Great Aunt Corrine would talk about my mother's 1st cousins, Wannona (Noni), Jean, & Ruth. When she talked about them I could listen to what she had to say and enjoy her stories as stories, even though I knew she was telling the truth. I learned early on that Noni was a sensitive and could feel things. I also learned that Jean was the 7th child and that she was born with a veil over her face – meaning that the baby comes out of the womb with the placenta covering their face – and this gave her an ability to see things and have premonitions.

My grandfather, John, was married 3 times, so I have 3 grandmothers (don't worry – you'll get it in a minute). My Maternal grandmother, Gloria, was his 1st wife, and my mother, Connie, is their child.

My 2nd grandmother, also Gloria, was his second wife and my Aunts Joanne, Saundra, Jacqueline (Jackie), and my Uncle John (Bunky) are their children.

My 3rd grandmother, Marge (Grandma Margie) was his 3rd wife and my Uncle Jason and my Aunt Renee are their children. When I was 16, I left Yonkers, NY and went to live with them in Liberty, NY.

My maternal grandmother, Gloria, died first. My 2nd grandmother, Gloria, died years later, and my grandfather died after his 2nd wife died. My Grandma Margie is still alive.

I learned from my grandfather, Grandma Margie, and my 2nd grandmother that my Great Aunt Birdie had a brother named Billy that would haunt my Aunt Joanne, Saundra, & Jackie every night after he died. My Uncle Bunky confirmed my grandfather's stories of how my aunts would open the curtains and be scared because they'd see his ghost outside their bedroom window on the 2nd floor. I also learned that my mother broke her arm when she was a child and when she was dancing around the next day, my grandfather asked her if her arm hurt and she told him no because Uncle Billy fixed it.

I was living back in Yonkers when my Grandma Margie got her wings and emerged from her cocoon as a beautiful butterfly. I'm not sure when or how it happened, but we were there for each other in a way nobody understood, and we didn't care. When I would talk about where I went with Grandma Margie, instead of being told I was weird, the response was simply, "Oh..."

The first thing that happened was Anthony Robbins' book, Awaken The Giant Within. Grandma Margie told me about him and about this book so I bought the book and read it – and I really got it! I was excited! I couldn't wait to tell her! Next was the fire walk – a 3-foot fire walk – this happened on a Tony Robbins weekend and it was phenomenal! Walking on hot coals wasn't a drug-induced cult – it was an experience that let you know if you can walk on fire, you can do anything you put your mind to! We got t-shirts from that weekend and I couldn't wait to wear my shirt to work the following Monday. My manager asked me about the t-shirt and I told him about my weekend as well as the supervisors. One of the supervisors told my manager, "Oh this is great – at the next manager's meeting all the managers will talk about their secretaries and you'll say well my secretary walks on fire!" My manager and I laughed and laughed at that one.

At this point, my Grandma Margie and I were more like besties than we were grandmother and granddaughter. We went to psychic fairs, we got readings, took pictures of our auras, played with pendulums, phoenix cards, laughing yoga, reiki, astrology, numerology, reflexology, essential oils, and more. Grandma Margie studied to become a psychic and she is also a certified reiki master. She would give me and my husband readings and reiki every time she came to visit – and if you were there, you could have one too. One night we sat in the Parkside Diner until 5 a.m. because Grandma Margie was giving readings to customers. I stretched out in the booth and took a nap at about 2 a.m. and when I woke up at 5, she was still giving readings.

Christine Varon has been my friend for many years. After she left New York, we lost touch until she found me in Facebook and sent me a friend request along with a message. I knew she knew me and, as always, I looked at her profile to see who our mutual friends were and that's when it clicked! I accepted her request right away and told her about my books.

Chris popped up in my timeline often and I always liked or responded to her posts. One day, I saw a post about a live show she was having on Friday night. I had no idea what the show was about but I like to support my friends, so I told my husband I was going to watch her show – and I was in awe! I wanted everything I saw! I made new friends! I laughed! I had fun!

I've been a customer of C2 Gems & Minerals for months now. I started thinking about writing a 'Crystal' book and just as I was thinking about it,

Chris told me she wanted to end up in one of my books. Obsidian Heart is that book.

This story is going to be thrilling, exhilarating, erotic, and maybe a bit psychotic? We'll see.

"What are you doing in here?!" he asked as he stormed into the room...

"I... I'm sorry..." I said as I put the sphere back in place...

"Come with me..." he commanded as he turned and walked out the room. I followed behind him, dreading what was coming as I went inside his office and sat down...

"Mr. Heart – please don't fire me – I..."

"Call me Sid..." he interrupted as he sat down behind his desk...

"Okay... Sid..." I was so nervous I started shaking...

"Amber – relax – I just want to talk..."

"Okay... Sid..."

"Your name is pretty..." I sat there for a few moments before I responded. I had an eerie feeling and I wasn't sure where this was going, so I kept my guard up as I replied...

"Thank you..."

"You're welcome – may I ask who named you?"

"I knew it!" I thought to myself... "Why?"

"My name is Obsidian..."

"Like the crystal?'

"I was named after my father, and he was named after his father..."

"Who named your grandfather?"

"My great grandmother..."

"She was into crystals?"

"My great grandmother was a psychic – she was into crystals, gems, essential oils, and reiki..."

"Oh wow..."

"The gem stones, tumbles, and spheres you've been playing with have been in my family for generations..."

"Oh wow – no wonder I feel so much energy from them..."

"You feel energy from them?"

"Yes..."

"What's it feel like?"

"I play with them in my hands... and they get warm..."

"That's energy alright..."

"Why does everybody call you Sid?"

"Because that's all they need to know..."

"My grandmother named me Amber..."

"Was your grandmother into crystals?"

"Yes – especially after she started going to see a psychic..."

"Your grandmother used to see a psychic?"

"Yes – that's when she got into the crystals – she started collecting them and when I turned 16, she gave me an amethyst sphere for my birthday..."

"So that's why you've been playing with it..."

"You've been watching me?"

"Yes... I've been watching you..."

"Oh my God – I wish I'd never gone in there..."

"I'm glad you did..."

"Why?"

"The crystals needed you..."

"Huh?"

"I'm not crazy!" he laughed...

"Okay... if you say so..."

"They always tell you to talk to your plants – right?"

"Yes..."

"Well – it's the same with crystals..."

"Really?"

"Oh yea – my great grandmother used to tell me that the crystals needed a home, they needed sunlight, and they needed to be cleaned..."

"So you gave them a home, you gave them sunlight..."

"And I clean them once a week..."

"So you walk in the room... clean them, and then you leave?"

"Pretty much..."

"Now I'm glad I go in there..."

"I am too..."

"I don't understand why you were watching me though..."

"I have cameras in the room to make sure no one steals any of them..."

"You thought I was stealing?!"

"No Amber – every time someone goes in the room, the cameras record..."

"Oh..."

"I came in here one day, I turned on my phone, and I saw I had 8 recordings – I started watching them... and I was fascinated... with you..." Oh boy. I wish he hadn't said that because I got really uncomfortable...

"Ummm... I'm going to go now..." I said as I got up to leave...

"Please don't go Amber – I didn't mean..."

"Yes you did..." I said as I left his office...

"What the hell did I just do?" he sighed as he put his head in his hands...

"I'm going home..." I said out loud as I went back to my desk. I logged off the computer, I locked the desk, and when I turned around, he was standing there...

“See you tomorrow?” I could tell by the look on his face he was hoping I would say I was coming back...

“See you tomorrow...” I confirmed. The fact that he smiled at me when I left actually made me feel worse.

"Hi Honey..." Jade greeted as she threw her arms around her husband and kissed him...

"Hey..."

"How was your day?"

"I had a good day..." he sighed as he took off his shoes and went to sit down in the recliner...

"You want a drink?"

"Yea..."

"Coming right up..." she said as she went to make him a glass of cognac on ice. Sid watched his wife make the drink and unbeknownst to her, he started thinking about me... "Sid!"

"Huh?"

"Where'd you go? I've been standing here holding your drink!" she laughed...

"Oh – sorry – I was just thinking..." he answered as he took the drink from her...

"I made steak & potatoes for dinner – let me know when you're ready to eat..." she said as she smiled at him mischievously...

"Okay..." he replied, looking out the window. He never noticed the hurt look on his wife's face...

"Amber! Hey!" Chris greeted as she answered me on messenger...

"Hey..." I sighed...

"How's the new job?"

"I thought I was goin' to get fired... but now that I know I'm not getting fired... I might quit..."

"Okay – what happened – the last time I talked to you, you really needed a job – you were so happy you got the job – how do you go from thinking you're going to get fired to wanting to quit?"

"Hold on – le'me get something to drink..." I said as she followed me into the kitchen. Chris watched me pour myself a goblet of moscato, put the bottle back in the refrigerator, pick up the phone, pick up the goblet, and go sit back down...

"Okay – take a sip, and tell me what happened!" she laughed...

"The manager's name is Sid Heart..." I stopped to take a sip before I continued...

"Sid Heart – as in Heart Tech?"

"Yea – how'd you know?"

"I know somebody that used to work there..."

"Well... Sid has this room on the floor that I've been going into..."

"A room? Like a supply room?"

"It's more like a ballroom..."

"A ball room? Really?"

"It reminded me of the Lounsbury House in Ridgefield – but instead of tables, the room has recessed lighting, deep-gold wainscoting on the walls, a deep-yellow and cream couch... and crystals..."

"I'd be in that room every day!" she laughed...

"I've been in there every day and today, he came in the room and asked me what I was doing..."

"Did he say the room was off limits?"

"No – but there is a sign on the door that says do not enter..."

"Oh Amber..."

"I told him I was sorry – but he said come with me..."

"Okay – you didn't get fired – so why do you want to quit?"

"We had a really deep conversation..."

"Hold on – now I need a drink!" she laughed as she got up. I waited for her to come back and I saw her goblet...

"What's that?"

"Sparkling Chardonnay – go 'head!"

"So he asked who named me Amber and when I asked him why, he told me his full name is Obsidian..."

"Ooohhh..."

"So we're talking, and he tells me his great grandmother name is grandfather Obsidian, his grandfather named his father Obsidian, and his father named him Obsidian..."

"Oh wow..."

"That's what I was thinking too – he told me the crystals and gems belonged to his great grandmother – they've been his family for generations..."

"That's nice!"

"I thought so too – he told me his grandmother was a psychic, she was into crystals, gems, essential oils, and reiki..."

"All this sounds really good – I still don't understand why you might quit..."

"I'm getting to that..."

"Okay..."

"So I told him my grandmother started seeing a psychic and then she started collecting crystals – and when I turned 16, she gave me an amethyst sphere for my birthday..."

"She did?"

"Yes – so then he says oh so that's why you've been playing with it..."

"He's been watching you!"

"Exactly!"

"Well – in his defense – the sign said do not enter..."

"I told him I wish I'd never gone in there – he says I'm glad you did..."

"He has a sign that says do not enter – you've been going in the room – he's been watching you – he's glad you went in the room because he likes watching you..."

"Exactly – first he said the crystals needed me – but then he told me he was fascinated with me..."

"See – that's a problem – especially because he's married..."

"I know he's married – but when he told me he was fascinated with me, I liked it..."

"Oh Amber..."

"I know, I know – that's why I got up and left..."

"You did the right thing..."

"I know that's what I supposed to do... but that's not what I wanted to do..."

"Oohhh..."

"I've been feeling energy from the crystals... and I've been feeling energy from him..."

"Oh my God – you didn't tell him that – did you?"

"Hell no – but now that we had that conversation, I feel better..."

"You feel better? I don't get it..."

"I didn't understand why I was feeling this energy from him before we had that conversation..."

"Do you still want to quit?"

"I don't want to quit – but I might need to..."

"Ohh... you're feeling him..."

"Yea... and he's feeling me too... and he's married..."

"Exactly..."

"And I'm going back to work tomorrow..."

"You just told me you might quit!" she laughed...

"I know..."

"I can't with you!" she laughed...

"Honey – what's wrong?" Jade asked...

"Nothing..." Sid answered as he continued eating without picking his head up to look at her..."

"Sid!" she exclaimed as she slammed her fork down on her plate...

"What?!" he exclaimed as she slammed his fork down too...

"Now that I have your attention..." she said as she got up from her chair, went over to him, and sat down next to him... "Tell me what's bothering you..."

"I'm sorry – I just can't stop thinking about her..."

"Her? Oh... I see..." she laughed...

"It's not what you think..." he lied...

"Honey – I know all about her..."

"You do?"

"You have cameras linked to the computer in your office – every time she went in that room I saw her..."

"Oh – I forgot about that..."

"You must've thought she was stealing from you..."

"I did..." he lied...

"Why didn't you tell me?"

"I didn't think you'd be interested..."

"Honey – just because I'm not interested in crystals, that doesn't mean I'm not interested in what's going on with you..."

"Thank you..."

"You can talk to me about anything..."

"She's been going in that room all week..."

"I know..."

"She plays with them, she talks to them, and she feels their energy..."

"Okay – let me stop you – rocks don't have energy..."

"See – this is why I didn't want to talk to you..."

"I'm sorry – I won't stop you again – go ahead..."

"Never mind..." he sighed as he got up from the table...

"Where are you going?"

"I'm going to bed..."

"I'll be up after I put the dishes in the dishwasher..." she said as he went upstairs...

"I don't give a damn what he says – rocks are just that – rocks – I don't care what color or shape you make them – maybe I'd have more energy if you concentrated more on getting me that diamond upgrade you promised me instead of trying to tell me that those damn crystals have energy!" she mumbled under her breath. When she was finished, she went upstairs and saw her husband was already in bed, so she took off her clothes and climbed into bed with him... "Honey..." she whispered as she spooned him and began kissing him on the back of his neck...

"Jade..."

"Yes Sid..." she breathed as she moved her hand down to his dick and took it in her hand...

"I'm not in the mood..." he said as he took her hand off his dick and turned his back to her. This was a pattern between them and Sid was tired. Every time he brought up the crystals she make a slick comment, he'd get upset, and then she would make it up to him by giving him sex – but tonight was the first time he decided to put a stop to it – and it wouldn't be the last.

"Good morning..." Jade breathed in Sid's ear...

"What time is it?" he groaned as he rubbed his eyes...

"It's a little after 5..." she breathed as she turned him over on his back and began kissing her way down his chest to his stomach...

"Why'd you wake me up... so... early..." he panted as he began playing in her hair as if he didn't know shy she woke him up. This was another pattern between the two of them – Jade knew her husband always woke up with a hard-on – and she also knew he preferred her mouth to a hand job any day – and ever since they said 'I Do' she hasn't missed a day... "Jade..." he moaned as she took his dick in her mouth all the way down to his balls... "Oohh... Shit..." he moaned. This was another pattern between the two of them. Sid knew whenever he was upset with her, she would put it on him good – and this morning, he was ready for it... "Yeesss... Suck it... Shit..." This was music to Jade's ears but unbeknownst to Sid, this morning was going to be a little different... "Why'd you stop?" he asked as he sat up...

"Ssshhh..." she whispered as she pushed him back down on the bed, straddled him, and sat on his dick. Sid was disappointed until she started bouncing up and down...

"Oh Sid... Yes... Fuck me..." Sid grabbed her ass and slammed her down on his dick as he thrust himself up inside her... "Yes... Oh God... Sid... Sid..."

"Ugh! Ugh! Ugh!"

"Sid... I'm cumming... I'm cumming..."

"Ugh! Ugh! Ugh! Ugh!"

"Huh! Huh! Huh! Huh!" Jade lay down on Sid while he was still inside her and kissed him... "I love you..."

"I love you too..."

"You want breakfast before you go to work?"

"Naa – it's early – I'll just take coffee..."

"I'll go make you some coffee..." she said as she got up off him...

"Jade – wait..." he said as he got up out the bed...

"Yes Sid?

"Come take a shower with me..."

"Okay..." Jade was elated that Sid asked her to come shower with him but what she didn't realize was that he asked her to take a shower with him to take his mind off of me...

"Good morning – thank you for calling Heart Tech..." I answered...

"Good morning – may I speak with Mr. Heart please..."

"Hi Mr. Osgood – he's not in yet..."

"Hi Amber – how are you?"

"I'm good – thank you for asking..."

"You're welcome – please have him call me..."

"I sure will – oh wait – he just came in - Mr. Heart – Mr. Osgood is on the phone for you..."

"Thank you – I'll take it in my office..."

"Bazil – what can I do for you?"

"I have a proposal for you Sid..."

"Oh boy – I'm listening..."

"It's not bad!" Bazil laughed...

"Bazil – I know you well enough to know that you don't do anything for anyone out of the kindness of your heart..." Sid laughed...

"Now see – I'm hurt..."

"I'm sorry – go 'head..."

"I told my wife your story..."

"My story?"

"I told my wife about your name, your crystals, and how they've been in your family for generations..."

"Oh boy – she thinks I'm crazy – right?"

"Not at all – in fact – my wife loves crystals..."

"Really?"

"I know – I was just as surprised as you are..."

"Oh wow – how do you feel about that?"

"If my wife told me she loved shit on a stick – I'd go get her some – as long as she didn't bring it in the house!"

"Bazil!" Sid laughed... "I can't!"

"When I died – my wife died – she came after me – she begged God for my life – and here I am – so if crystals make her happy, I'm all for it – which brings me to the reason I'm calling you..."

"Wait – wait – wait – you never told me you died!"

"I'll get back to that another time – let me tell you why I'm calling!"

"Okay, okay!" Sid laughed...

"My wife wants to publish your story..."

"What?!"

"My wife says there are a lot of people that are interested in crystals and she'd love to publish your story..."

"Oh my God – I don't believe it!"

"So are you interested?"

"I need to think about it..."

"Check your email..."

"Why?"

"My wife asked her cover designer to make a cover – take a look at it and then let me know what you think..."

"Okay Bazil – thanks..."

"You're welcome..." Bazil said as he hung up...

"Amber – could you come in here please?"

"Sure Mr. Heart – I'll be right there..." I answered as I got up and went into his office...

"Close the door..."

"I'm not sure that's a good idea – I don't want anyone telling your wife I'm in your office with the door closed..."

"There's no one else here..."

"I'd rather leave the door open..." I said as I went to sit down and he stopped me...

"Wait – come over here – I want to show you something..."

"On your computer?"

"Yes..."

"Okay..." I said as I went behind the desk and bent down... "Oh my God!" I thought to myself as I caught his scent... "What am I looking at?" I asked, snapping myself out of my thoughts...

"This is an email from Beautiful Publications..."

"Beautiful Publications?"

"Yes – that's a publishing company under Osgood Publishing..."

"Oh my God! You're writing a book?!"

"His wife wants to publish my story..."

"Oh Sid – that's great! Congratulations!"

"Thank you..."

"Open it!" I exclaimed...

"Okay, okay!" he laughed as he opened the email and we both looked at the cover...

Beautiful Publications Presents
Obsidian
HEART

"Oh my God! That cover is fire!" I exclaimed...

"It is nice..."

"Is that your wife?"

"Yes..."

"How'd they get your picture?"

"Bazil and his wife were at our wedding..."

"Ohhh..."

"He must've given this picture to his wife..."

"His wife owns Beautiful Publications?"

"Yes..."

"Looking at this cover, she makes me want to write a book..."

"Really?"

"Yes!"

"How would you feel about being in this book?"

"Me? Why me?"

"Because..." he said as he stood up... "You're part of my story..." he breathed as he pulled me into his arms and kissed me. I knew I should've pushed him away but he felt so good I didn't want him to stop, so I put my hands around his back as we continued kissing..."

"Sid? Are you here?" Jade called out, startling us both..."

"I'm in here!" Sid answered, giving me time to adjust myself...

"There you are!" she said as she came into the office...

"Hi Mrs. Heart..." I greeted...

"Hello Amber..."

"What brings you down here?" Sid asked as I went to sit back at my desk...

"You left your briefcase at home – I thought you might need it..."

"Thank you – I didn't realize I left it home...

"Have you had lunch?"

"Not yet..."

"C'mon – I'll take you to lunch – my treat..."

"Sounds good to me..." he said as he got up from his desk. I turned to see them walking out of his office holding hands... "Amber – we're going out to lunch – I'll be back later..." he said as they left...

"Thank you Lord..." I sighed...

"Where are we going?" Sid asked...

"Boca Oyster Bar..." she answered as they got in the car and drove off. When they got to the restaurant Sid got out the car, opened the door for Jade, and they walked into the restaurant arm in arm...

"Welcome to Boca – table for two?"

"Yes..." Jade answered...

"Right this way..." the hostess said as she escorted them to a table out by the water...

"This is nice..." Sid said...

"You're welcome..."

"Welcome to Boca – my name is Tamika – may I start you off with something to drink?"

"I'll have a glass of Chardonnay..." Jade answered...

"Will that be Lincourt or Talbott?"

"Talbott..."

"And you sir?"

"I'll have the Riesling, Barth..."

"Would you like any appetizers?"

"Yes – we'll have fried calamari, clams casino, boca ceviche, and filet tips..." Jade answered...

"Okay – I'll be right back with your drinks..." the waitress said as she walked away...

"How'd you find out?" Sid asked...

"Find out what?"

"You didn't get a call from Bazil?"

"No – why – is something wrong?"

"Here's your drinks – your appetizers will be out shortly..." the waitress interrupted as she put the drinks on the table and walked away...

"You have perfect timing – hopefully we'll be celebrating..." Sid answered...

"Le'me guess – Beautiee's pregnant again..." Jade laughed...

"Beautiee wants to publish my story..."

"Oh wow! That's great Honey! Congratulations!" she exclaimed as she pulled him into a kiss...

"Thank you..."

"So when did you sign the contract?"

"I haven't given them an answer yet..."

"Why not?"

"Let me show you the cover..." he said as he pulled It up on his phone and showed it to Jade...

"Oh... I see..." she sighed...

"Here's your food..." the waitress interrupted as she began putting the food on the table...

"That looks really good..." Sid said...

"If you need anything else, I'll be over there..." the waitress said as she pointed across the area...

"Thank you..." Sid said. When the waitress walked away, he continued... "Jade – what was that supposed to mean?"

"Sid – please calm down..."

"Answer my question..."

"I thought it was going to be a story about Heart Tech..."

"Beautiee doesn't write or publish books about computers..."

"Exactly – she writes erotic fiction – how do your crystals fit into that category?"

"Does it matter?"

"I guess not..." she sighed...

"Bazil said she has a lot of readers that would be interested in my story..."

"He said that?"

"Yes..."

"She is something else..." Jade laughed as she put some food on her plate...

"What's that supposed to mean?"

"She must like crystals too..."

"As a matter-of-fact – she does..."

"I just don't get it..."

"That makes two of us..." Sid said as he put some food on his plate...

"What's that supposed to mean?"

"I just don't get why you can't be happy for me..." he sighed...

"You know what – I've lost my appetite..." she said as she got up...

"So you're leaving?"

"I'll see you later..." she answered as she left...

"Is everything alright?" the waitress asked...

"Everything's fine..." Sid sighed...

"You didn't eat anything..."

"I know – my wife had an emergency – could you please pack everything up to go?"

"Sure – I'll get this packed up – and I'll bring the check..."

"Bitch invites me to lunch –her treat – and I'm paying the check..." he laughed as he shook his head...

"Here you go – have a great day..." the waitress said as she put the bag on the table along with the check...

"Here you go – have a nice day..." Sid said as he put cash in the bill holder...

"Thank you – you too..."

"Thank God you're back – I'm starving!" I exclaimed as Sid came in the door...

"You like seafood?"

"Yes..."

"Come with me..." he said as he went down the hall towards the crystal room...

"We're eating in here?" I asked...

"Yes – take the food out – I'll be right back..." he said as he hurried out the room...

"Okay!" I exclaimed as I opened the bag... "Ooohhh – Boca!" I exclaimed as I took all the food out and put the tins on the table...

"Here..." Sid said as he put a plate in front of me... "Help yourself..."

"Thank you!"

"You're welcome..." he said as he sat down. I put some of everything on my plate and waited...

"Why are you waiting?"

"I'm waiting for you to get some food..."

"I thought you were starving?"

"I am!"

"Go ahead and eat..." he laughed as he put some food on his plate and then we both started eating...

"So what did your wife think?"

"She didn't..."

"Sid..." I said as I put my hand on his... "I'm sorry..."

"I'm going to call Bazil and tell him I don't want to have my story published..."

"Umm... you can't do that..."

"I've already made up my mind..."

"I need to tell you something..."

"Okay..."

"Mrs. Osgood called while you were out..."

"What did she say?"

"It's not what she said... it's what I said..."

"What did you say?"

"I told her you loved the cover..."

"Amber – you shouldn't have done that..."

"I didn't mean to – but she asked me if you had a chance to look at it... I told her you showed it to me... and then I told her you loved it..."

"It's fine..." he sighed...

"Why don't you want to do it then?"

"My wife thought it was going to be a story about my company..."

"I wouldn't read that..."

"You wouldn't?"

"Nope – but I'd read the story about your crystals..."

"You know what? I'll do it!"

"Yes!"

"Here's to Obsidian Heart..." I said I picked up a clam...

"To Obsidian Heart..." he said as he picked up a clam and then we both sucked them down... "I'm going to call Bazil right now..." he said as he got up..."

"Congratulations..."

"Thank you..." he said as he left the room. I started cleaning up and just as I was about to leave the room, I remembered he had cameras in there...

"Hello Sid..."

"Hello Bazil..."

"Have you seen the cover?"

"I have..."

"What'd you think?" Bazil asked as he put the phone on speaker...

"I loved it!"

"So you'll do it?"

"I'll do it!"

"My wife will be very happy to hear that..."

"Do you need me to do anything else?"

"Come by our office tomorrow morning..."

"Can I make it tomorrow afternoon? Around 2 p.m.?"

"That'll work..."

"Okay great – I'll see you tomorrow..." Sid said as he hung up...

"Yes!" I exclaimed as I went running over to him and hugged him. He pulled me into a kiss again and this time, he started pushing me backwards towards his desk...

"Sid... we can't..."

"Yes..." he breathed as he laid me down on his desk... "We can..."

"Sid... No..."

"Okay..." he sighed as he stepped back and helped me up off his desk...

"I'm sorry..."

"You have nothing to be sorry for..."

"I want you... but..."

"Did you just say you want me?" he interrupted...

"Yes..." I sighed...

"That's all I need to know..." he said as he kissed me on the cheek and left.

"Hey Amber..."

"Hey Chris..." I sighed...

"Oh no – what happened?"

"Why do I want this man so bad?" I sighed as I put my head in my hands...

"Amber... you didn't..."

"I didn't... but I wanted to..."

"Amber... Nooo..."

"I can't help it – when I'm near him – I can't explain it – I've never felt like this..."

"I think I know what's happening..."

"You do? Please tell me – I need to know I'm not going crazy..."

"Tell me what happened – and don't leave anything out..."

"I went to work..."

"I know that!" she laughed...

"Mr. Osgood called and said he needed to speak with Sid..."

"Okay..."

"So Sid came in, I told him Mr. Osgood was on the phone, and he took the call in his office..."

"Okay..."

"After he got off the phone with Mr. Osgood, he called me in his office..."

"Uh oh..."

"He said he wanted to show me something on his computer..."

"Uh oh..."

"I bent down to see what he wanted to show me..."

"Uh oh..."

"I felt his energy... he smelled so good..."

"Amber!"

"He opened an email from Mrs. Osgood at Beautiful Publications..."

"Oh thank God!"

"Don't thank him yet..." I laughed... "Mrs. Osgood wants to publish his story..."

"Oh wow! That's great!"

"I thought so too – especially after he showed me the cover - they sent him the cover to his book and we love it..."

"We?"

"Yes – that's what he wanted to show me..."

"Oh – I thought you were going to tell me something else..."

"I am..."

"Oh no – what happened?"

"He asked me how I would feel about being in his book and when I asked him why, he said I was a part of his story... and he kissed me..."

"He's in love with you..."

"I kissed him back..."

"You're in love with him..."

"His wife walked in..."

"Oh my God!"

"The only reason we didn't get caught is because she went down the hall to the crystal room..."

"That was supposed to happen..."

"Huh?"

"You're being protected – she was sent down the hall so you wouldn't get caught..."

"That doesn't make any sense!"

"Hold on a minute..." she said as she got up and went over to her table...

"What's that?" I asked as I looked at the deck she was holding...

"These are Phoenix Cards..."

"Phoenix Cards?"

"Yes – I'm going to give you a reading..."

"With Phoenix Cards?"

"Yes – they're going to tell me if you and Sid were in a past life together..."

"Ooohhh..."

“Have you ever had a reading like this before?”

“Yes – I didn’t take it seriously though...” I laughed...

“Why not?”

“I just did it for fun...”

“What did the cards say?”

“The cards said me and my grandmother had 2 past lives together...”

“Really?”

“Yes – and get this – in one life, I was her son – in the other life, I was her husband!” I laughed...

“Aaaah Haah Haah Haah! “Aaaah Haah Haah Haah!”

“I know!” I laughed...

“Okay – I’m going to put these cards into four piles – I want you to pick from one pile and then I’ll tell you about the cards you picked – if you’re drawn to two groups of cards, it means you’re a combination of the two groups...”

“Okay...” I watched her put the cards in piles and then I picked... “Okay – I’m definitely drawn to group 3 – but I’m also drawn to group 1...”

“Okay – I’ll do group 3 first...” she said as she moved the other piles to the side and pulled the 1st card... “Mountains – this means you were very grounded. You provided for a family, you were an important role for others, you were their rock - people needed to trust you...”

"That sounds nice..." I said as she pulled the 2nd card...

"Protection Guardian – Life may have hardened you – you developed a tough exterior – maybe you were hurt a lot so you felt the need to be the protector and the strong one, you guarded your emotions..."

"That sounds a lot like my life now..." I said as she pulled the 3rd card...

"Princes of Summer – this is definitely you – you were very sensitive, kind, and open-hearted – but you were also inexperienced – you found it hard to let people in - people didn't know this side of you because you may not have let them in..."

"That does sound like me..." I said as she pulled the 4th card...

"Legend – You were a person who learned from ancestors. You may be tuning into this reading because you're always interested in lessons you can learn from those before you – you had people you looked up to and you were happy to learn from – you're a student of life – you've always been happy to learn new things – always looking into self-development..."

"That's cool – and true..." I said as she pulled the 5th card...

"Unicorn – oh my God – this is so you - very colorful, very eccentric, very open to magic, spirituality, and positivity – a life full of surprises, serendipity – full of magic because you allowed magic in..."

"Aaaah Haah Haah Haah! "Aaaah Haah Haah Haah!"

"What's so funny?"

"I'm picturing myself as a unicorn!"

"Okay – now I'm going to do group 1..." she said as she pulled the 1st card... "The Seer – this is also you – you were very spiritual in a past life but because it was dangerous to speak on it you kept it to yourself – you didn't speak on being psychic. There's also a psychic streak in ancestry – you were ready before your time..."

"That's definitely true..." I said as she pulled the 2nd card...

"Hunter – You were active and fearless. You were the head of the tribe. You were the head of the family. You were determined and strong, but you also went through a lot – you have some battle wounds – but you're proud to wear them..."

“How did you know this?”

“I didn’t pick the cards – you did...” she said as she picked the 3rd card... “Queen of Spring – oh yea – I can see this too – you were very independent, charming, and talented – and that carried over into this life – In this past life you had a hi ranking – you were very important – you were a leader – you had big aspirations and dreams – you weren’t afraid to do what you wanted...”

“That has definitely carried over into this life!” I exclaimed as she picked the 4th card...

“Potential – Okay – the Queen of Spring & Potential cards picked together is significant - You had lots of potential; however, you never reached your full potential – maybe something tragic happened to cause your life to end before you could reach your full potential or maybe people weren’t agreeing with you as a person – this explains why your independence, charm, and talent carried over into this life...”

“Wow...” I said as she pulled the 5th card...

“Competition – You were seen as competition, a threat to others. People were threatened by your intuition. You were fearless.

You had a very charming, talented aura - you didn't live a regular life..."

"Do you have any popcorn?"

"Yes – why?"

"Go make yourself some popcorn..."

"Oh damn – okay – I'll be right back!" she exclaimed as she got up. I waited for her to come back and when she sat down, she had a huge red bowl of popcorn... "Okay – I'm ready..." she said as she started eating...

"I hurried up, adjusted myself, and I went back to my desk..."

"Oh – okay..."

"She told him he left his briefcase home and she thought he needed it..."

"That was nice..."

"She asked him if he had lunch, he said no, so she said she would treat him to lunch, and they left..."

"That was nice!"

"No – it wasn't..."

"How do you know?"

"He came back to the office with a bag of appetizers from Boca..."

"Maybe he just wanted to buy you lunch..."

"No – there's more..."

"Uh oh..."

"We ate together in the crystal room..."

"Okay..."

"I asked him what his wife thought about the book and he said she didn't..."

"Oh no..."

"He said he was going to call Mr. Osgood and tell him he wasn't going to do the book, but I talked him into it..."

"You did? How?"

"Mrs. Osgood called while they were at lunch and she asked me if he had a chance to look at the cover, so I told her he did, he showed it to me, and we loved it..."

"Did you tell him that?"

"Yea..."

"How'd he feel about that?"

"He said I shouldn't have done that..."

"I agree..."

"He was so excited when he saw that cover, he was so passionate when he told me I was a part of his story, he was so passionate when he kissed me – I know he wants to do this!"

"He's conflicted..."

"Maybe he was conflicted – but after this afternoon, I don't think he's conflicted anymore..."

"Amber..." she said as she came closer to the screen... "What are you saying?" she asked as she raised an eyebrow at me...

"Well... we ate lunch, we both picked up a clam, we toasted to his book, we sucked down the clam, we went in his office... and..."

"Uh oh... I'm not sure I like where this is going..."

"Let's just say I'm glad there aren't any cameras in his office..."

"Amber – did you have sex with him?"

"Almost..."

"How do you almost have sex with somebody?"

"We started kissing again, he started pushing me backwards, I told him we can't, he pushed me down on his desk, and he said yes we can..."

"Oh my God – he tried to rape you?!"

"No..."

"Oh thank God!"

"I said no, he stopped, he helped me up off the desk, I told him I was sorry, and he said I had nothing to be sorry for... but...."

"What?"

"After he told me I had nothing to be sorry for, I told him I wanted him..."

"What?!"

"Yea..."

"What'd he say?"

"He said that's all he needed to know, he kissed me on the cheek, and then he left..."

"Oh my God – I can't!" she exclaimed with tears in her eyes... "I need to do a reading for him – you two belong together!"

"I'm going to call you tomorrow on facetime so you can see him and do a reading..."

"Okay – keep me posted – I have plenty of popcorn!"

"Thanks for meeting with me..." Sid said as he went into Bazil's office...

"You're welcome – but my wife's gone for the day..."

"That's good – 'cause I need to talk to you..."

"What's wrong?"

"I want a divorce..."

"Sid! No! What happened?"

"It's not what happened – it's what's been happening – today was the last straw..." he sighed...

"Well what's been happening?"

"My wife never loved me for me..."

"That's not true – your wife loves you very much..."

"She only loves part of me – she doesn't love all of me..."

"Is this about the crystals?"

"Yes..."

"You're going to leave your wife over crystals?"

"You don't understand..."

"Make me understand – I'm all ears..."

"You told me when you died, your wife died too – she pleaded with God for your life..."

"Yes..."

"I asked you how you felt when you found out your wife was into crystals – do you remember what you said?"

"I said if my wife told me she loved shit on a stick I'd get her some – as long as she didn't have it in the house..." Bazil laughed...

"You'd be willing to get your wife shit on a stick if she wanted it – and my wife isn't even willing to accept my crystals – that's why I keep them at the office..."

"You keep your crystals at the office? You don't keep your crystals in your house?"

"No..."

"That's crazy! We have a library in our house – my wife has her books and her desk on one side – I have my books and my desk on the other side..."

"See? I can't even do that!"

"Are you sure? Did you ever ask her?"

"Every time I try to talk to my wife about my crystals she interrupts me – we get into it – I get mad – we don't speak – and then she makes it up to me by sucking my dick and giving me pussy until the next time..."

"Why does she interrupt you? Why doesn't she just listen?"

"Because she doesn't want to hear it..."

"I'm sorry – but are you sure you want a divorce?"

"Yes..."

"What happened today that made you want a divorce?"

"Well – if I'm being honest – there were a few things that happened before today too..."

"Tell me..."

"I hired a receptionist – Amber..."

"Okay..."

"So after she started working for me, I noticed I had eight videos on my phone..."

"You have surveillance cameras..."

"Yes..."

"Okay..."

"I started watching them – I saw her playing with and talking to my crystals..."

"Ooohhh..."

"Last week I asked what she was doing in there and I asked her to come to my office..."

"Did you fire her?"

"No – I never wanted to fire her – I wanted to talk to her..."

"Okay..."

"So we got in a really deep conversation – I told her my full name is Obsidian and she says like the crystal – I told her the crystals have been in my family for generations – I told her my grandmother was a psychic. She told me her grandmother named her Amber – her grandmother went to see a psychic – her grandmother collected crystals, and when she was 16 her grandmother gave her an amethyst sphere for her birthday..."

"Can I say something?"

"Sure..."

"Amber is filling a void – she's giving you something you need – something you're not getting from your wife..."

"I know..."

"Are you sure that's enough reason to file for a divorce?"

"Let me finish..."

"Okay..."

"I told Amber I saw her playing with the crystals, so she knew I was watching her – and then I told her I was fascinated with her..."

"Oh no..."

"I know – but I can't help it..."

"You need to get rid of her..."

"I don't want to get rid of her – I think I love her..."

"You know you sound crazy – right?"

"Yes..."

"When did you fall in love with her?"

"I knew I loved her from the moment I kissed her..."

"What?! You kissed her?!"

"You called me earlier today..."

"Okay..."

"You told me to check my email..."

"Okay..."

"I called Amber into my office..."

"Why?"

"I wanted to show her the cover..."

"Did you show her the cover?"

"I did – and she loved it – so I asked her how she felt about being in the book and when she asked me why I wanted to put her in the book, I told her because you're part of my story – and I kissed her..."

"Are you serious?!"

"She kissed me back..."

"Ooohhh..."

"We were kissing when my wife came in..."

"Oh my God! Your wife caught you?"

"No..."

"Oh thank God!"

"My wife brought me my briefcase and then she told me she was taking me to lunch – her treat..."

"Oh thank God!"

"Don't thank him yet..."

"Oh no – what happened?"

"We went to Boca – I asked her how she found out..."

"We never told your wife..."

"I know – I told her we had something to celebrate – I told her your wife wanted to tell my story – she congratulated me, she kissed me – I was so happy..."

"How'd you go from that to wanting a divorce?"

"I showed her the cover – and her entire demeanor changed!"

"Why?"

"She thought Beautiee wanted to do a story on Heart Tech..."

"My wife doesn't publish that genre..."

"Exactly – so my wife says so how do your crystals fit into erotic fiction – so I told her Beautiee said she has readers that would love to read my story – so my wife says oh – let me guess – Beautiee likes crystals too..."

"Damn man – I'm sorry..."

"So I said as a matter-of-fact – she does – and my wife says I just don't get it – I said that makes two of us – so she says what's that supposed to mean – so I said I just don't get why you can't be happy for me – this Bitch tells me she's lost her appetite, gets up from the table, and leaves!"

"What?!"

"Thank God I work downtown so I was able to walk back to work..."

"I'm really sorry..."

"And get this – she didn't pay the check either!"

"Oh shit!"

"So I paid the check, I packed up all the food, I took it back to the office, and had lunch with Amber..." he said as he started smiling...

"Uh oh..."

"I was going to call you and tell you I wasn't going to do the book, but Amber already told Beautiee we saw the cover and we loved it..."

"You were really going to call us and tell us you didn't want to do the book?"

"Yea..."

"Why were you going to do that if you really wanted us to publish your book?"

"I was going to do that for her..."

"I'm glad you decided to do it..."

"I'm glad Amber talked me into it..."

"So how was lunch?"

"Lunch was great – Amber made me feel so much better – we ate - we picked up clams - we toasted to my book - we sucked down the clams – and then we went back to my office and next think you know – I had her on her back on my desk..."

"You fucked her?!"

"I would've if she didn't stop me..."

"Yea – you're crazy..."

"I'm not so sure about that..."

"I'm sure!" Bazil laughed...

"She told me no so I helped her up off the desk – she apologized – I told her she had nothing to be sorry for – and then she told me she wanted me..."

"Oh my God..." Bazil whispered...

"I asked her did you just say you wanted me – she said yes – I told her that's all I need to know, I kissed her on the cheek, and now I'm here..."

"So you're in love with Amber?"

"Bazil – I thought you of all people would understand!"

"Me?"

"You fell in love with Beautiee the moment you saw her..."

"Yes I did – but that was different..."

"You were going from woman to woman – you were never interested in anything but pussy – but once you found Beautiee – all of that changed..."

"You're right – but I wasn't married..."

"Would it have mattered if you were?"

"Honestly?"

"Honestly..."

"Probably not..." Bazil sighed... "Does your wife know about Amber?"

"My wife knows Amber was in my crystal room playing with my crystals – but she doesn't know I kissed her..."

"Oh so you told her about Amber?"

"She saw Amber in my room playing with my crystals..."

"She did? How?"

"I have the cameras connected to my computer at home – whenever it records, it goes on my computer, so she watched the videos..."

"Thank God you didn't kiss her in there!" Bazil laughed...

"Right!" Sid laughed... "So I told my wife I couldn't stop thinking about how Amber was playing with the crystals and feeling their energy, and she says – wait – let me stop you – rocks don't have energy..."

"Oh damn..."

"So I went to bed – she gets in bed – she's kissing on me – she takes my dick in her hand – I take her hand off my dick, tell her I'm not in the mood, turn my back on her, and go to sleep!"

"Beautiee tried that one time – and I fixed her ass!" Bazil laughed...

"Really?! What happened?!"

"We got into it when she was pregnant so she went to sleep in the guest room – and she locked the door so I couldn't get in..."

"Oh my God!" Sid laughed...

"That's alright – I waited for her to leave the house, I took the door off the hinges, and I left a letter apologizing to her on the bed so when she got home, she'd see it..."

"Aww – damn!"

"Aww damn is right – she read that letter and we fucked the shit out of each other!" Bazil exclaimed...

"I know that's right – did you ever put the door back on the hinges?"

"Oh yea – we turned that into Jay's room..."

"I can't imagine you not being with her..."

"I can't either..."

"Well – my story ended the way it usually does – she woke me up early, sucked my dick, gave me some pussy, and then I went to work..."

"You don't sound too happy about that..."

"I'm not..."

"You don't enjoy making love to your wife?"

"I don't want her to suck my dick and give me pussy because she knows she fucked up – I want her to suck my dick and give me pussy because she loves me and she wants me..."

"I feel you on that..."

"Now I gotta go home and tell her..." Sid sighed...

"Are you sure you wanna do this?"

"Yea..." Sid answered as he got up and left...

"Oh Shit! He's having lunch with Amber!" Jade whispered as she watched Amber and her husband on the video... "Shit – look how happy they are – I really fucked up this time..." she sighed as she continued watching... "That should've been us..." she sighed... "Honey – I'm sorry... I'll make it up to you – I'm going to make it up to you starting tonight..." she said as she got up and went downstairs to the kitchen...

"Daddy!" the kids yelled as Bazil came in...

"Wait a minute..." Bazil said as he knelt down so they could run towards him. Beautiee came around the corner as they knocked him down on his back and smothered him with hugs and kisses...

"Alright – let your father get up..." she laughed...

"Okay Mommy!" Lydia said as she got up off him...

"C'mon Daddy – I'll help you get up... Uggh!" Jay exclaimed as he tried to help Bazil up only to fall back down on the floor...

"Aaah Haaa Haaa Haaa – Aaah Haaa Haaa Haaa!" they all laughed. This was their special routine every day and Beautiee never interrupted it. Sometimes she'd take out her phone and take pictures of them all on the floor laughing at each other...

"Okay – let me get up..." Bazil said...

"Okay Daddy..." they all said as they got up off him one by one...

"Daddy!" Beautiee exclaimed as she threw her arms around him and kissed him..."

"Hey – we need to talk..."

"Jay – go turn on the television – Daddy needs to talk to Mommy..."

"Okay – come on..." Jay said to his brother and sisters...

"Mommy – can we go upstairs and watch television?" Joy asked...

"Sure..."

"Okay!" the girls squealed as they ran upstairs...

"Jay – are you going upstairs or are you staying down here?"

"C'mon Joseph – let's go upstairs..." Jay said as he went upstairs and Joseph followed him...

"Come into the library..." Bazil said as he took Beautiee by the hand and led her into the library...

"What's wrong Bazil?"

"Sid came to see me tonight..."

"I thought we told him tomorrow?"

"We did – but he wanted to talk to me about something else..." Bazil sighed as he sat down...

"What's wrong?"

"He wants a divorce..."

"What?! Why?!"

"Jade never accepted his crystals..."

"They're getting divorced over crystals?"

"He said whenever he wants to talk to Jade about the crystals, she interrupts him – basically, she doesn't want to hear it..."

"Oh damn..."

"He hired a new receptionist named Amber..."

"Okay..."

"She's been playing with crystals – he has camera's in the room so he's been watching her – he called her into his office and they had a deep conversation – her grandmother went to see a psychic, her grandmother collected crystals, and her grandmother gave her an amethyst sphere for her birthday when she was 16..."

"Oh wow..."

"Sid told Jade that Amber played with the crystals and felt their energy – Jade interrupted him and told him rocks don't have energy..."

"See – I hate that shit – I'm glad you don't do that to me Baby..." Beautiee said as she kissed him...

"After you begged God for my life, stood by me when my parents came back from the dead, and helped me help them get back to the afterlife in peace – I'm the lucky one..." he breathed as he kissed her...

"I'm sorry they're getting a divorce though..."

"Me too – but I understand it..."

"You do?"

"After I spoke to him yesterday Jade showed up to take him to lunch..."

"Oh so that's why he was out when I called...

"Yea – and they got into it – and she left him at the restaurant..."

"Oh my God! Why?!"

"She thought you wanted to do a book about Heart Tech..."

"What difference does it make? I want to publish his story – why can't she just be happy for him?"

"That's what he said..."

"I hope he doesn't change his mind..."

"He was going to – but Amber changed his mind..."

"Amber?"

"Yea – he had lunch with her – she reminded him how much he loved the cover – so they celebrated..."

"Oh my God – are they having an affair?!"

"I don't think so – but between you and me – he loves her..."

"Oh shit!"

"Also – between you and me – he told her she's a part of his story..."

"I don't know whether I should be happy for them or sad for Jade..." Beautiee sighed...

"I know..."

"Thank God I'm not going through any of that with you..."

"Never..." Bazil breathed as he kissed her...

"I hope he doesn't change his mind again..."

"He's telling Jade he wants a divorce tonight..."

"I'd be devastated if you told me you wanted a divorce..." Beautiee sighed...

"Listen to me..." Bazil said as he took her face in his hands and kissed her... "I... will... never... ever... leave... you... do... you... understand... me?"

"Yes..." Beautiee laughed between kisses... "Yes... I... understand... you..."

"Jade?"

"I'm in the kitchen..."

"Jade – we need to talk..." Sid said as he sat down at the table...

"We sure do – I'm so sorry for the way I acted – I never should've left you at the restaurant - I'll make it up to you..."

"That won't be necessary..."

"So you forgive me?"

"Yes – I forgive you..."

"Oh Sid!" she exclaimed as she hurried over to the table and threw her arms around him...

"Sit down Jade..."

"Okay..." she sighed as she sat down next to him..."

"There's no easy way for me to say this..."

"Say what?"

"I want a divorce..."

"What?!"

"I want a divorce..."

"Are you serious?"

"Yes..."

"Unbelievable!"

"Are you really that surprised? It's not like we've been getting along all that great lately..."

"You want a divorce over some got-damned rocks? Really?"

"I want a divorce because I wanted you to love me for me..."

"I do love you for you!"

"My crystals are a part of me – a part that you refuse to acknowledge or accept..."

"I do acknowledge that your crystals are a part of you – I'm just not into them..."

"It's more than that – you don't even listen to me when I talk to you about them..."

"So you want a divorce because I won't let you convince me that rocks have energy – you know what – I can't!"

"That's exactly my point!"

"What's that supposed to mean?'

"I was offered a book deal – why couldn't you just be happy for me?"

"You're right..."

"That doesn't answer my question..."

"I know – I'm sorry – c'mon – let's go upstairs – I'll make it up to you..."

"No thank you..."

"Excuse me?!"

"I said no thank you..."

"Are you serious right now?!"

"As a matter-of-fact – I am..."

"Can't we get past this?"

"I don't want you to suck my dick and give me pussy because that's how you apologize whenever you fuck up – I want you to suck my dick and give me pussy because you love me and you want me..."

"You know what?! Fuck you!!" she exclaimed as she took off her wedding rings, threw them on the table, and stormed out the kitchen...

"Good morning..." Jade breathed as she started kissing Sid on the back of his neck. Sid got up out the bed, put his robe on, and went to take a shower without speaking. Jade got up out the bed and went to get in the shower with him but when she tried to open the bathroom door it was locked so she went downstairs and started making coffee. Sid got out the shower, got dressed, and came downstairs into the kitchen... "I made coffee..."

"Thanks..." he said as he made a container to go. When he started to leave, Jade stopped him...

"Sid – wait..."

"Yes Jade?"

"Is it really over between us?" she asked with tears in her eyes...

"I'm afraid so..." he answered as he went out the door...

"I can't believe it's come to this..." she sighed as she made herself a cup of coffee, went upstairs, and went into his office... "Le'me watch this again..." she said as she started watching the video again... "Wait a minute – what the fuck is this?!" she exclaimed as she stopped the video and zoomed in... "She's holding his hand – this Bitch is fucking my husband!!" she exclaimed as she got up and went to take a shower...

"Good morning..." Sid greeted...

"Good morning..." I replied...

"We need to talk..."

"Okay..." I sighed as I got up and followed him into his office...

"Come here..." he breathed as he pulled me into a kiss...

"Sid... Stop..." I breathed as I tried to push him away...

"I told my wife I wanted a divorce..." he said, still holding me...

"Wait – what?!"

"I told my wife I wanted a divorce..."

"Are you serious?"

"Yes..." he breathed as he kissed me again... "Did you mean what you said yesterday?"

"Yes..."

"I want you too..." he breathed as he kissed me again...

"I don't want to start anything as long as you're married..." I breathed as we continued kissing...

"I know... and I respect that..."

"Okay..." I breathed in his mouth as he kissed me hard...

"Promise me you'll wait for me..."

"I promise I'll try..." I breathed as we continued kissing...

"You promise you'll try? That's the best you can do?"

"Yes..."

"Okay – I'll take that... for now..."

"Good – 'cause I need to talk to you..." I said as I let go of him and I went to sit in the chair...

"What's wrong?" he asked as he sat down in the chair next to me...

"I've been talking to my friend Chris about you..."

"You've been talking about me?" he asked as he smiled at me...

"Yes..."

"What have you been telling your friend?" he asked as he leaned closer to me...

"Well... I told her about you, your crystals, how I've been playing with them, feeling their energy, and also feeling your energy..."

"Wow... I don't know what to say..."

"I needed her to help me understand why I was drawn to you – I needed her to help me understand why I want you as much as I do..."

"Did she help you understand why you want me?" he asked as he took my hand in his...

"Yes... and no..."

"I don't understand..."

"Well... Chris gave me a reading with Phoenix Cards..."

"Phoenix Cards?"

"Yes – they tell you about your past lives..."

"How'd your reading go?"

"Well... she said she wants to do a reading with you..."

"Me? Why?"

"She wants to do a reading with you so she can compare your past lives with mine to see if we've had any past lives together..."

"Ooohhh..."

"Will you do it?"

"Sure – I'll do it – I'm curious to see what she comes up with..."

"Can I call her now?"

"Yes..."

"Okay!" I squealed as I pulled up my messenger and called Chris on video...

"Good morning!!!" Chris sang...

"You're in a good mood!!" I exclaimed...

"Yes I am!"

"I have news..."

"I still have popcorn!" she laughed...

"Sid agreed to a reading..."

"Really?! Is he there?!"

"I'm here!" Sid said as he snatched the phone from me...

"Hello Obsidian! It's nice to meet you! I've heard a lot about you!"

"Yes you have..." Sid laughed...

"Okay – I want to go over what's going to happen – I took a deck of phoenix cards – I put the cards in four piles – yesterday I did a reading for Amber – today I'm going to use the same four piles to do your reading – Amber did you tell him what pile you picked or anything about your reading?"

"Nope..."

"Good – Sid I'm going to put the four piles on the table – I want you to pick a pile..." she said as she put the piles in front of her...

"Okay – I'm drawn to pile number 2..."

"Okay – are you drawn to any other piles?"

"Yes – I'm also drawn to the first pile..."

"Okay!" Chris said as she smiled...

"You picked the first pile too – didn't you?" he asked as he smiled at me...

"Yes..."

"Okay Sid – we're going to do pile number 2 first..."

"Why'd you ask me to pick a second pile?"

"I didn't ask you to pick a second pile – I asked you if you were drawn to a second pile..."

"Okay – why?"

"I always ask that question when I do readings because if you're drawn to more than one pile, it means you're a combination of the two..."

"Oh... Okay..."

"Okay – now I'm going to start with pile 2..." she said as she pulled the 1st card... "Summer – in a past life you lived in warmer climate – you loved warmth and happiness..."

"And now I'm living in one of the coldest areas..." Sid laughed...

"You were nurturing, maybe a mother, hard worker, basked in joy..."

"I was a mother?"

"I know – in past lives it's possible to be a male in one and a female in another..."

"Oh that's crazy!" Sid laughed...

"It is – I had a reading with my grandmother - in one life I was her son – and in the other life I was her husband!" I laughed...

"Oh shit!" Sid laughed...

"She Wolf – Mega wild side!"

"That's definitely me!" he laughed..."

"You're more responsible in this life - but in your past life you lived on the wild side – you lived life to the fullest – you did what you felt was right....

"That's true..." he said...

"King of Spring – You were very inspiring, and ambitious. You had a leadership role - people looked up to you but this caused a lot of drama. You were born into a prestigious family, but you didn't like being in the spotlight so there were times you may have rebelled against it..."

"I think that carried over into this life..." he said...

"Here's where it gets interesting..."

"Okay..."

"You and Amber both picked group one – in that group one of the cards is Queen of Spring – you were both very independent, charming, talented, and hi ranking – you were both very important, you were both leaders, you had big aspirations and dreams, and you weren't afraid to do what you want..."

"Are you telling me I was a King and a Queen?" Sid laughed...

"No Sid – you picked pile 2 first – King of Spring came up first – Amber was your Queen..."

"My Queen..." Sid sighed as he took my hand and kissed it...

"Okay – that's from the 1st pile – now I'm going to get back to your 2nd pile..." she said as she pulled another card... "Face Your Fears – You always wanted to have a good time – you didn't let fear get in your way – this maybe how your life ended, but it ended in a beautiful way – you lived life to the fullest..."

"With My Queen..." he sighed...

"I'll get back to that..." she said as she pulled another card... "Leadership – You set goals, you were born into leadership – you were the decision maker in your life – you basked in joy...."

"With My Queen?" he asked...

"Okay – now I'm going to do pile 1..." she said as she pulled the 1st card, deliberately ignoring his question... "The Seer – this is also you and Amber – you were both very spiritual in a past life but because it was dangerous to speak on it you kept it to yourself – you didn't speak on being psychic. There's also a psychic streak in your ancestry – you were ready before your time..."

"That's definitely true..." he said as she pulled the 2nd card...

"Hunter – You and Amber were both active and fearless. You were the head of the tribe. You were the head of the family. You were determined and strong, but you went through a lot – you have some battle wounds – but you're proud to wear them..."

"I ruled with My Queen..." he sighed. Chris didn't comment as she picked the 3rd card...

"Queen of Spring – I told you about this earlier..."

"Yes..." he sighed as he took my hand and kissed it...

"Here's where it takes a turn..." she said as she turned over the next card...

"Potential – okay – whenever this card is picked following the King of Spring or the Queen of Spring it's very significant - You both had lots of potential; however, you never reached your full potential – maybe something tragic happened to cause your lives to end before you could reach your full potential or maybe people weren't agreeing with you..."

"So we were dethroned..." Sid sighed...

"Possibly..."

"When you picked this card for me yesterday I thought the potential referred to my talents..." I said...

"It does – but I believe it also refers to you both as King & Queen..." Chris said...

"I think so too..." Sid sighed as Chris pulled the next card...

"Competition – You were both seen as competition – you were both seen as a threat to others – this is why I think the Potential card referred to you as King & Queen..."

"Wow..." Sid whispered...

"People were threatened by your intuition. You were fearless. You had a very charming, talented aura - you didn't live a regular life..."

"Now I know why I want you so much... My King..."

"Now I know why I want you so much... My Queen..." he breathed as he pulled me into a kiss...

"Oh my God – I can't wait to tell Chandra about this – you guys have to invite me to your wedding!" Chris exclaimed as she started crying...

"Where the fuck is she?!" Jade exclaimed as she stormed in...

"What the hell?!" I exclaimed as she stormed into his office...

"Bitch – you're fired – get the fuck out – now!"

"Can she do that Sid?" I asked...

"Stop talking to him – I said get the fuck out!" she exclaimed as she came towards me and attempted to grab my arm...

"Don't put your hands on me!" I snapped...

"You have two choices – you get the fuck out – or I'll call the police and have you escorted out!"

"I'm leaving..." I said as I got up...

"That's your best bet!" she snapped as I got my things and left...

"Was that his wife?!" Chris asked...

"Oh shit – I thought you hung up!"

"I was about to..."

"Yea – that's his wife..."

"Maybe it's a good thing you got fired – after what I told you, you don't need to work there anyway..."

"You're right – especially since he asked his wife for a divorce..."

"What?! Oh shit!!"

"Yea..."

"That's why she fired you..."

"Yea..."

"I'll look around – send me your resume..."

"I will thanks..."

"You're welcome – I gotta go – keep me posted..."

"I will..."

"Have you lost your got-damned mind?!" Sid exclaimed...

"Did you really think you were going to fuck her right under my nose?!"

"What the hell are you talking about?!"

"Oh please – I know you're fucking her!!"

"I'm not fucking anybody!!"

"Whatever – she better not come back here!"

"This isn't your company - I can hire whoever I want!"

"Guess again – we never signed a pre-nup – I own 50 percent – you can't do shit without me!"

"We'll see about that!" Sid exclaimed as he got up, walked past her, and stormed out of his office...

"While you see about that..." Jade hissed as she went into the kitchen and pulled out the can of turpentine... "I'll see about this!" Jade's eyes turned to slits and she smiled a sinister smile as she went down the hall towards the crystal room...

"Oh shit – I forgot to give them back their key!" I exclaimed as I stopped suddenly... "Fuck it – I'll go back - put the key on Sid's desk – and leave!" I said as I turned to go back towards Sid's office...

"Since these fuckin' crystals are so important to you – let's see how you feel after your precious rocks are returned to coals and ashes!" she laughed as she pointed the can towards the curtains and began spraying the turpentine on them...

"Hmmm – Jade's car is still in the parking lot – she must still be upstairs – oh well – I'll knock on the door and just let her know I'm dropping the key off – I don't even have to talk to Sid..." I said as I hurried upstairs...

"Now let's move on to these ugly-ass walls!" she exclaimed as she pointed the can towards the walls and started spraying the turpentine on them...

"Hello? Sid? Jade? Anybody here?" I called out as I opened the door and let myself in... "I just came back to leave the key!" I yelled as I put the key on the front desk... "What the hell is that smell?" I asked as I went down the hall towards the crystal room... "Oh my God!! The crystals!!" I shrieked when I saw the flames...

"Didn't I tell you not to come back here Bitch?!" she growled...

"Jade – the crystals..."

"Since you both love these fuckin' crystals so much – you can burn in hell with them!" she growled as she ran out the room and locked me in...

"Oh God – help me!" I cried as I dialed 911...

"911 – What's your emergency?"

"She set the fire – Heart Tech – she locked me in – I can't get out – I'm trapped!"

"Where are you Maam?"

"Heart Tech... Behind... The... Courthouse!" I coughed as I dropped the phone... "Crystals..." I coughed as I broke the lock on the display case and began shoving the crystals, gemstones, and spheres in my bag...

"This is Sid Heart..."

"Mr. Heart – we're dispatching the fire department to your building..."

"Oh my God – what happened?!"

"We received a 911 – a woman was shrieking – the woman said she set the fire – she's trapped inside..."

"Oh God AAAMMMBBBEEERRR!!" he cried as he hurried back towards his building...

"Thank God you're here!" Jade exclaimed...

"Did you call 911?" the fire chief asked...

"Yes – this is my husband's company – please hurry!"

"The caller said she was trapped inside..."

"Yes I was – I couldn't get the door open..."

"So there's no one else inside?"

"Not that I know of..." she lied...

"Chief – we're inside – the fire started in a room down the hall..."

"Is there anybody in there?"

"We can't tell yet – there's too much smoke!" The fire chief shook his head as he called 911...

"911 – What's your emergency?"

"This is Chief Johnson – we're responding to the fire at Heart Tech – where did that call come from?"

"Chief – the line is still open..."

"What?!"

"The caller never hung up – we're still connected..."

"Guys – get in that room – the caller's still in there!"

"We're in here Chief – we got her – she was under the table..."

"Is she alive?"

"She's alive..."

"Oh my God – where's Amber?!" Sid exclaimed as he ran up to the fire chief...

"They got her..."

"Is she alive?!"

"She's alive..."

"Oh thank God!!" he exclaimed as they brought me down on the stretcher...

"Mr. Heart?"

"Yes – I'm Mr. Heart..."

"We responded to a 911 – the caller said she set the fire – she was trapped – she couldn't get out..."

"Chief – we're gonna get her to the hospital..." one of the firefighters said as they put me in the ambulance..."

"I need you both to come with me down to the police station..." the fire chief said...

"That's fine..." Sid agreed...

"Why do we have to go to the police station – isn't it obvious what happened?!" Jade exclaimed...

"What happened Jade?" Sid asked...

"I told the Bitch not to come back – she came back and set your office on fire..."

"Why would she do that?" Sid asked...

"Because I fired her – Duh!!"

"Let's go down to the police station..." the fire chief said...

"Yes Jade – he's right – we should go file a police report – she should be arrested as soon as possible..." Sid said...

"Fine..." Jade sighed...

"Chief – I'll ride with you..." Sid said...

"My car's right here..." Jade said. Sid ignored her and got in the SUV with the chief...

"You have something you wanna tell me?" the chief asked as he started the engine...

"My wife set that fire..."

"I know she did..." he agreed as they headed towards the police station...

"We have a fire victim!" the firefighter yelled as the ambulance pulled into the hospital..."

"How's she doing?" the doctor asked...

"She's breathing – but she inhaled a lot of smoke..."

"Is she conscious?"

"I think so..."

"Is that her bag?"

"Yea..."

"Let's see if we can get an I.D...." the doctor said as he went in the bag... "Amber Morrison..." he read off my job I.D. as I turned my head... "Amber – I'm Doctor Preston – I want you to blink if you can understand me..." I felt silly blinking my eyes, but I did it anyway... "We're going to do an EKG, we're going to send you for a CT scan, and I'm going to listen to your chest and see how you're breathing – okay?" I shook my head yes... "Guys – can we take the oxygen mask off?"

"Sure..." one of the firefighters answered as he came over to me and took it off...

"Thank... you..." I coughed...

"I don't like the sound of that – we need to get you on oxygen..." Dr. Preston said...

"She... set... the... fire..." I coughed...

"Chief Johnson – what can I do for you?" Sergeant Corbett asked...

"You can hurry up and make an arrest so she doesn't get away with it..." Sid answered as Jade came in...

"Come with me..." Sergeant Corbett said as they followed him into his office and sat down...

"We responded to a 911 at Heart Tech – the caller said she was locked in, she was trapped, and she couldn't get out..."

"I was the caller..." Jade lied....

"Hang on..." Sergeant Corbett said as he took out a pad and proceeded to write a report. They all watched as he wrote and when he stopped, she continued... "I called 911 to tell you Amber set the fire..." she lied...

"Uh huh – go 'head..." Sergeant Corbett acknowledged as he continued writing...

"You said you were trapped – but then you were able to get the door open and get out..." Chief Johnson said...

"Yes – that's correct..." Jade lied...

"Hmmm – that's interesting because before we left, I placed a call to the 911 dispatch and they said the call never disconnected – and this was while I was standing outside with you..."

"I didn't set the fire – Amber did!" Jade exclaimed...

"Okay – hold on!" Sergeant Corbett yelled... "Why would she set the fire?"

"Because I fired her!"

"Uh huh..." Sergeant Corbett acknowledged as he wrote...

"I told that Bitch don't come back – she came back – she set the fire – and she got caught!"

"I know how we can settle this..." Sid said...

"Really? You gon' tell me how to do my job?" Sergeant Corbett snapped...

"I was just going to suggest that since my wife was in the building and she's insisting that Amber is the one that set the fire, my wife should be willing to let you swab her hands to prove she had nothing to do with it..."

"Sid!" Jade exclaimed...

"You know what – that's a great idea!" Sergeant Corbett agreed as he stood up...

"I'm not going anywhere or giving you anything!" Jade exclaimed...

"You don't have to – but this isn't just about arson – once I confirm what the chief is saying – it's also about attempted murder – I can arrest you and hold you for at least 24 hours – once you're place under arrest – I don't need your consent to swab your hands, your clothes, your car – or anything else I want to swab..."

"Okay – it was an accident – I just wanted to burn those fuckin' crystals – she came back to drop off the key – she came down the hall looking for you – I got out once the fire started – she didn't make it out..."

"So you lied to me when I asked you if anybody else was in the building!" Chief Johnson exclaimed..."

"Jade Heart – you're under arrest for arson and the attempted murder of Amber Morrison..."

"Who the hell did I marry?" Sid whispered...

"Sid – I'm sorry – it wasn't supposed to be like this – please – don't leave me!" she cried as Sergeant Corbett led her by the arm to be processed and Sid left the precinct with Chief Johnson. When they got to the processing room, Sergeant Corbett gave Jade the Miranda warning:

1. You have the right to remain silent.
2. Anything you say can and will be used against you in a court of law.
3. You have the right to an attorney.
4. If you cannot afford an attorney one will be provided for you.
5. Do you understand the rights I have just read to you?"

"I understand..." Jade sighed as she began to cry...

"With these rights in mind, do you wish to speak to me?"

"No..."

"MY name is Gert – I'll be processing you. You'll take off your clothes, you'll squat, you'll cough, and then you'll be escorted to the shower. After you take a shower, you'll put on this jumpsuit and you'll be brought back here. You'll receive an Inmate ID, an Inmate Number, and an Inmate Handbook – I suggest you take the time to read the manual so you know what's expected of you. I'll be right back…" she said as she walked away to speak to someone else… "Alright Jade – come with me..." Gert said as she took Jade to a room with a private shower… "Take off your clothes…"

"Can I have some privacy?" Jade asked...

"Squat and cough." Gert commanded, ignoring Jade's question. Jade did as she was told... "Take a shower and put on this jumpsuit..." she said as she handed Jade the jumpsuit. Jade took the quickest shower she's ever taken, dried off, and put on the jumpsuit. "C'mon..." Gert said as she took Jade by the arm and escorted her back to where she was processed. "Here's your Inmate ID, your Inmate Number, and your Inmate Handbook – read it or not – time to go to your cell..." she said as she took Jade by the arm again and brought her to her cell. On the way down, Jade saw other ladies in their cells... "Here's your cell – the doors stay open for a while – the common area's over there – they'll be an announcement when it's light out – once they make that announcement, everyone is to return to their cell for the night – welcome to prison..." Gert said as she turned and walked off.

"Sigh... I might as well sit down and get comfortable..." Jade said as she sat on the hard bed, picked up the Inmate Handbook, and started reading. The first she noticed was the handbook was 42 pages...

"Damn..." she said out loud... "Oh well – at least I won't be bored..." she said out loud as she read the mission statement...

"The Bridgeport Correctional Center shall protect the public, protect staff and provide safe, secure and humane supervision of offenders with opportunities that support restitution and rehabilitation by providing meaningful programming designed to support successful community re-integration..." Jade flipped to the table of contents and scrolled down to Addressing Staff, Following Orders, Personal Conduct, and Personal Safety – page 6 – and she paid particular attention when she got to Personal Conduct...

"You are required to conduct yourself in a responsible manner. A. You are not permitted to engage in behavior that disrupts the order of the facility, threatens security, endangers the safety of any person or imperils state or personal property. B. You are not permitted to make sexually suggestive remarks or gestures to any person. C. You are not permitted to make excessive noise or to use profanity..." She shook her head and started reading the paragraph under Personal Safety...

"If you believe that your safety is at risk, report your concerns to a staff member immediately. The Department of Correction and this facility are committed to ensuring your safety..." Jade glanced at the Clothing/Accessory, Personal Hygiene, Housing Unit rules, Fire Safety, Movement and Corridor Regulations and stopped to read what was outlined under Dining Hall...

1. You will have five (5) minutes after chow call to leave the unit before you are late. Being late will cause you to miss chow.
2. Cutting in line is not permitted.
3. You are responsible for receiving a complete tray; only one (1) trip through the serving line is allowed.
4. You are required to sit in the seat next to the last occupied seat at each table. Skipping seats is not permitted.
5. No items may be taken into the dining hall except your own utensils; no items may be taken from the dining hall.
6. You must eat with your housing unit or work detail.
7. You will have twenty (20) minutes to eat your meal.
8. You must take your tray to the scullery after you finish your meal and scrape it into the proper container provided.
9. You must leave the dining hall after you finish eating and proceed to your housing unit or assigned area.

Jade started crying when she got to page 22 and read paragraph A. under the Mail Section...

"You may correspond and receive an unlimited number of correspondences at your own expense. You may write to anyone except: a victim of any crime you have been convicted of or in which disposition is pending…"

"Well – I guess that means I can't write to Sid or Amber..." she laughed as she continued reading. When she got to page 25 and read the paragraph under Initial Visit it made me feel even worse...

"You may receive two (2) adult visitors from your immediate family pending completion of processing your visiting Application Form or for seventy-two (72) hours after admission. You may add your two immediate family members to your visiting list after intake by submitting a request to your counselor. A back ground check will be conducted and they must have the same last name as you..."

"Nobody gives a damn about me..." she whispered as she cried...

"Visits between an inmate and their attorney or other credential individual from the community such as law enforcement officials, community agencies and program, shall normally be accommodated during the following time periods; 8:15am to 10:15 am, 12:45pm to 2:15pm and 6:30 pm to 10:30pm. Attorneys do not need to pre-schedule. All other professional visits need to be pre-scheduled through the Counselor

Supervisors Office. The visiting rooms for professionals will be assigned first come, first serve..."

"I hope I get a good attorney..." she sighed. She kept turning the pages until she got to page 28 and read the paragraph under Section H. – Telephone Regulations...

1. Telephone calls are only permitted between 9:00 a.m. and 10:30 p.m. (9:00-10:30am; 12:00-2:30pm; 7:00-10:30pm)
2. Five (5) calls a day of 15 minute duration are authorized.
3. You are not permitted to make third party calls or calls to Department of Correction officials or to a victim of a crime you are charged.
4. Telephone calls are not permitted during facility lockdowns.

Jade kept turning the pages until she got to page 29 and read the paragraph under Section 18. Court Trip...

A. You must wear your own clothing unless you have none, in which case you will wear the state-issue uniform.
B. By 4:00 a.m. of the day of court, you must have your personal property packed and your bed stripped. Take your property and your bedding, including towels, to the A&P Room. The facility is

not responsible for any property you leave behind in your housing unit.
C. You are only permitted to take legal materials with you that pertain to the case at hand. These materials must be surrendered to the transporting staff during transit. The materials will be returned to you when you are in secure lock-up at the court and, on the return, when you are back in the facility.
D. You will be subject to the use of restraints in accordance with Department policy. (Reference: A.D. 6.4, Transportation of Inmates).
E. A court lunch will be provided.
F. You are not permitted to obtain or receive any item from any person while on a court trip.

Jade groaned out loud when she got to page 30 and read Section 19. Orientation...

"The next business day after admission to this facility, you will be required to attend an orientation session. The purpose of these sessions is to inform you of how the facility works, what your obligations are, and what programs and services are available. Counselors will answer any questions you may have. If you refuse to attend orientation a Disciplinary Report will be given to you by your unit officer. Under normal circumstances you can expect to be housed in a designated orientation unit for at least seven (7) days after being admitted to this facility..."

Jade kept turning the pages until she got to page 33 and started reading Section 4. Speedy Trial...

"Speedy trial is a petition from an inmate to the court having jurisdiction to initiate proceedings to dispose untried charges. There are three types of speedy trials that affect inmates in custody; (1) an inmate in custody solely because of charges pending in this state (C.G.S. Sec. 54-82m); (2) an inmate under sentence with untried charges pending in this state (C.G.S. Sec. 54-82c); (3) an inmate under sentence with untried charges pending in another state (C.G.S. Sec. 54-186, Article III). To apply for a speedy trial under C.G.S. Sec. 54-82m, contact your attorney or initiate pro se. For the other speedy trial motions contact your counselor.

"Hmmmmm... maybe I can get a speedy trial..." she sighed as she closed the manual, lay down on the hard ass bunk, and closed her eyes...

"Who set the fire?" Dr. Preston asked...

"My wife..." Sid answered as he came in..."

"Who are you?"

"I'm Sid Heart – my wife set the fire at Heart Tech..."

"I'm Dr. Preston – your employee is lucky she made it out alive..."

"Yes she is..." he sighed as he came over to me and took my hand... "I'm sorry..." he breathed as he kissed me...

"Dr. Preston?"

"Yes Remi?"

"Isn't he married?"

"Who?"

"Mr. Heart..."

"Yes..."

"He's kissing Amber..." she whispered as she pointed towards us. Dr. Preston looked over at us, shrugged his shoulders, and went back to writing in his clipboard...

"Sergeant Corbett – what are you doing here?" Sid asked...

"I'm here to see Amber..." he answered as he came over towards me... "Amber – I need to take a statement from you..."

"Okay..." I coughed...

"Can you tell me what happened?"

"She... set... the fire..." I coughed...

"Did you see her set the fire?"

"I... went... back... to... return... key..." I coughed...

"Okay..."

"I... smelled... smoke..."

"Okay..."

"I... went... to... room..."

"Okay..."

"I... saw... fire..."

"Okay..."

"I... saw... Jade..."

"Okay..."

"She said... since... I... love... crystals... so... much... I... can... burn... in... hell... with... them..." I answered as I started coughing uncontrollably...

"Oh my God! She really tried to kill you?!" Sid exclaimed...

"She... locked... door... I... was... trapped..." I coughed as I started crying...

"Okay – that's enough..." Dr. Preston said as he came over... "Sergeant – are you done with my patient?"

"Yes – I got what I needed..." he answered as he got up... "Mr. Heart – I'll keep you posted..." he said before he left...

"Amber – I want to do an EKG – Mr. Heart – I need you to go back in the waiting area..."

"NO!" I coughed...

"You want him to stay?"

"Yes..."

"Okay – Mr. Heart – could you sit over there?"

"Sure..."

"Remi – could you bring in the cart so we can get the EKG?" Nurse Remi came in with the machine and came over to me...

"I'm Remi – this will be quick..." she said as she hooked me up, got the EKG, and waited for Dr. Preston to look it over...

"It's normal – thank you Remi..."

"You're welcome..." she said as she left with the machine..."

"Call Chris..." I said...

"I don't have her number..." Sid said...

"Call... her... on messenger..." I coughed...

"Where's your phone?"

"In... fire..." I answered as I started crying...

"Here – use mine!" Sid exclaimed. I took his phone, logged into Facebook, sent her a message, and waited...

"Hello?" Sid answered...

"Obsidian – this is Chris – where's Amber?"

"She's right here..." he answered as he handed me the phone...

"Amber – are you okay?"

"No..."

"Where are you?"

"St. Vincent's..."

"I'm on my way..."

'Here..." I said as I handed Sid his phone...

"Shit! I forgot!" Sid exclaimed as he called Bazil...

"Sid! I was beginning to think you forgot about us!"

"Amber's in the hospital..."

"Oh my God!! What happened?!"

"Jade tried to kill her..."

"Amber!" Chris exclaimed when she saw me...

"Chris..." I sighed. We both started crying as we hugged each other...

"I can't do this right now..." Sid said...

"Go..." I said...

"Amber – I don't want to leave you..."

"GO!!" I exclaimed...

"Amber... I..."

"Sid... please... I need to talk to Chris..."

"Okay – Bazil – I'm on my way..."

"What's going on?" Chris asked...

"You know me too well..."

"Yes I do..."

"Go in my bag..." Chris went to get my bag and when she looked inside, she gasped...

"Oh my God! Does he know?"

"No..."

"Are you going to tell him?"

"Not yet – I want you to take them and clean them..."

"I can do that..."

"She tried to kill me Chris..."

"Are you sure?"

"After I hung up with you, I remembered I still had the key so I went back there to give them their key..."

"Was she there?"

"I saw her car – I went into the building – I knocked on the door – nobody answered so I went inside – I called out to let them know I was dropping off the key – I was going to leave but I smelled smoke so I went down the hall – I saw the fire – I ran into the room – Jade came in – she said Bitch didn't I tell you not to come back here – all I could think to say was crystals – she said since you love these crystals so much you can burn in hell with them – she ran out – she locked the door...” By this point we were both crying... “I called 911 – I told them she set the fire – she locked me in – I was trapped – I couldn’t get out...”

“Stop...” Chris interrupted as she put up her hand...

“I broke the door on the display case – I grabbed the crystals – I threw them in the bag – I was choking – I couldn’t breathe – I thought I was going to die – thank God they found me...”

“You could’ve run... you risked your life... for him...”

“The door was locked – I was trapped – I thought I was going to die – I had to protect the crystals...”

“And you were willing to die trying!” Chris laughed...

“I know – crazy – right?”

“Not at all...”

“It’s okay – I know that was crazy...”

“I don’t think so...”

“Really?”

“You were supposed to go back there...”

“I was?”

“Think about it – Jade set the fire – you just happened to remember you didn’t give them their key – you just happened to smell smoke – you just happened to go in that room – you just happened to save these crystals, gemstones, and spheres from being burned – you just happened to have a bag big enough to hold everything – you just happened to make it out of the fire – with the crystals – without being burned...”

“I wasn’t going to die... I was being protected...”

“Exactly...”

“Sid – come with me...” Bazil said as he put his arm around Sid and escorted Sid to his office...

“Hi Sid...” Beautiee greeted...

“Hey Beautiee...” he sighed...

“Are you sure you want to do this?”

“Absolutely...”

“Start anywhere you want...” Beautiee said as she started the recorder...

“I went into work and Amber was there. I told her we needed to talk and I soon as I got her in my office, I started kissing her...”

“Are you having an affair with Amber?” Beautiee asked...

“Does it matter?”

“Yes...”

“Why?”

“My readers love the sex combined with drama...”

“Your readers may be disappointed...”

“Let me be the judge of that...”

"No I'm not having an affair with Amber – but I knew she was a part of my story from the moment I saw her – and she confirmed it after you sent me the cover..."

"Okay!" Beautiee exclaimed...

"You sound happy..." Sid laughed...

"I am happy – and my readers will be happy too..."

"Really? I thought you said your readers love the sex combined with drama?"

"They do – but my readers also love a faithful man that doesn't cheat – especially a Black man – go 'head..."

"Oh – okay – where was I – oh yea – I was kissing Amber..."

"Okay..."

"Amber told me she wanted me to stop so I told her I asked my wife for a divorce..."

"Oh! Drama! Okay! Go 'head!"

"Amber said she didn't want to start a relationship with me as long as I was still married and I told her I respected that..."

"Aww..." Bazil and Beautiee sighed..."

"I asked Amber to be patient and wait for me and she promised she'd try..."

"Aww... damn..." Beautiee sniffed as she wiped tears from her eyes...

"Amber said she had something she wanted to talk to me about so we sat down and she told me she'd been talking to her friend Chris about me..."

"She must really be feelin' you..." Bazil said...

"She said she needed Chris to help her understand why she was so drawn to me and why she wanted me so much..." Sid whispered as he teared up...

"That's beautiful..." Bazil said as he teared up too. Beautiee got the box of tissues, took one for herself, and then she passed the box to Sid as he continued...

"Chris told Amber she needed to give me a reading and compare it to Amber's reading to see if we had any past lives together..."

"Wait – past lives?" Beautiee asked...

"I'd heard about this from my great-grandmother – but when Amber told me she had a reading done – I knew I had to do it – I wanted to know..."

"Did you do it?"

"I did..."

"How was it?"

"Chris divided the Phoenix Cards into four piles – Amber picked the 3rd pile, I picked the 2nd pile, and we both picked the 1st pile..."

"Oh my God – I hope you get a print out or a recording of your reading – I have to include this in your story!"

"Chris told me that in a past life, I was a King, Amber was My Queen, and our lives had a tragic ending..."

"Oh my God – I can't!" Beautiee exclaimed as she burst into tears...

"Jade came storming into the office – she called Amber a Bitch, told her she was fired, and she wanted Amber to get the fuck out or she was going to call the police..."

"Where did all that come from?" Bazil asked...

"She thinks I'm fucking Amber..."

"Because you told her you want a divorce..." Beautiee said...

"Exactly..." Sid confirmed...

"I told Jade it was my company – I could hire whoever I wanted – she tells me guess again – there's no pre-nup – I own 50 percent of this company – I said we'll see about that – I stormed out – I was on my way here when I got the call that my building was on fire – Amber was trapped inside..." he said as he started tearing up along with Beautiee...

"You said your wife tried to kill her..." Bazil said...

"When I got there – Jade told the fire chief she was the one that called 911 – she was trapped but she was able to get the door open and get out – while she was lying to the chief the firefighters brought Amber out on a stretcher and put her in the ambulance..." Bazil put his arm around Sid and cried along with him as Beautiee was crying too... "We both knew Jade was lying so the chief suggested we go to the police station –

after we got there she kept insisting that Amber set the fire because she was angry she got fired – so I suggested that Sergeant Corbett should swab her hands for evidence to rule her out – that's when she admitted to staring the fire – she claimed it was an accident – she claimed she only meant to burn the crystals – she claimed she saw Amber inside but she didn't know Amber never made it out..."

"Oh my God – she really wanted to kill her..." Beautiee whispered...

"Chief Johnson called the 911 dispatch – Amber never hung up after she called 911..."

"Wait a minute – you had cameras in there!" Bazil exclaimed...

"Yes..." Sid confirmed...

"Don't you have a recording in your phone?"

"Yes..."

"Have you watched it?"

"I can't..." he whispered as he started crying...

"Take your phone to the police station – let Sergeant Corbett download the video from your phone..."

"I didn't think of that..."

"I want to put that in your story..." Beautiee said...

"NO!" Sid exclaimed as he shook his head back and forth...

"Not the video itself – I'll tell my readers how you couldn't bring yourself to watch your wife make an attempt on your Queen's life..."

"Okay..."

"I think you should watch the video..." Bazil said...

"No... I can't..."

"Don't you want to know how your Queen survived?"

"Well... now that you put it that way..."

"Give me your phone..."

"Okay – here..." Sid said as he took his phone out his pocket and handed it to Bazil...

"Sid – why don't you come with me to my assistant's office and go over your contract while Bazil looks at your video?" Beautiee asked as she stood up...

"Okay..." Sid agreed as he stood up and followed Beautiee into Joselyn's office...

"Hi Joselyn – this is Obsidian Heart..." Beautiee said as she introduced him...

"Hi – I'm Joselyn – I'm going to be the first one to get your autography..." she laughed as she got up to shake his hand...

"Nice to meet you Joselyn..." Sid said...

"I've printed out your contract – take your time – if you have any questions – ask Beautiee – I'll be right back..." Joselyn said as she left and went to the conference room...

"Oh my God! Sid needs to see this!" Bazil exclaimed as he hurried down the hall...

"I'm ready..." Sid said...

"Are you sure?! You don't want your attorney to look over your contract before you sign it?!"

"That won't be necessary..." Sid said as he signed his contract..."

"Sid – you have to see this!" Bazil exclaimed as he hurried into Joselyn's office...

"Bazil – can it wait? We need to bring Sid into the conference room..."

"Sure – it can wait..."

"C'mon Sid..." Beautiee said as she got up and Sid followed them to the conference room... "Sid – go inside..." Sid opened the door and was in awe...

"Surprise!" Everyone yelled...

"For me?!" he gasped as he started crying...

"Welcome to Beautiful Publications!" everyone said in unison as they all raised a glass of champagne. Sid got a glass of champagne and raised it...

"Thank you..." he said and then they all drank their champagne. They spent the rest of the afternoon drinking champagne, eating hors d'oeuvres, and celebrating...

"Jade Heart – please report to the visitor's room..." the warden announced over the loud speaker...

"What now?" Jade sighed as she went to the visitor's room and sat at an empty table...

"Are you Jade Heart?" the man asked as he approached her...

"Yes – who are you?"

"I'm your court-appointed attorney, Smalls..." he said as he extended his hand...

"I can't afford you..."

"Doesn't matter – you're entitled to representation – can we talk?"

"Sure..." she agreed as she stood up and shook his hand...

"Come with me..." Smalls said as he took Jade by the hand and led her to the attorney-client room...

"Is your name really Smalls?" she asked as he closed the door behind him...

"My name is Jackie Small – my friends and clients call me Smalls..."

"Okay... Smalls..."

"I have your file..."

"I'm guilty..."

"Do me a favor..."

"Okay..."

"Let me talk..."

"Are you telling me to shut up?!" she snapped...

"Yes..."

"Fuck you!!" she exclaimed as she stood up to leave...

"Sit the fuck back down!! Now!!"

"Excuse me?!"

"You heard me – don't make me repeat myself..."

"Alright - I'm sitting – now talk!!"

"Thank you – as I said – I have your file. I know you confessed, they have the 911 call, and they have the video..."

"The video?"

"Your husband had surveillance in that room..."

"Oh – right..."

"I'm known in Fairfield County as a mother fucker..."

"Really?!"

"Oh yea – the District Attorney can't stand my ass!" he laughed...

"Why?!"

"Because she can't beat me..."

"She'll win this one..." Jade sighed...

"No – she won't..."

"You did read my file – right?"

"Yes..."

"And you still think she won't beat you?"

"I know she won't..."

"Please tell me more – I'm all ears!"

"I'm advising you not to go to trial..."

"Why?"

"As you said – you're guilty..."

"Duh!"

"You're also married..."

"Yes – I am – but my husband wants a divorce..."

"Is that what set you off?!"

"Yea..."

"How long have you been married?"

"Two years..."

"Is there a pre-nup?"

"No..." Jade watched as Smalls smiled...

"You're smiling..."

"Yes I am..."

"I'm intrigued..."

"Well – for starters – I would say your best bet is to plead this out..."

"I've been charged with arson and attempted murder..."

"As I said – I'm known in Fairfield County as a mother fucker – I can bring them a deal where you agree to plead guilty to 2nd degree arson and 2nd degree attempted murder – that carries a sentence of 7 to 10 years instead of 20 to life..."

"Did you say 20 to life?!"

"1st degree arson is 7 to 10 years – 1st degree attempted murder is 15 to life – you do the math..."

"Oh God – I can't do life in prison!!"

"Exactly – and if you plead this out – you won't have to..."

"Are you sure?"

"I read your confession, and I watched the video. From what I saw, it wasn't pre-meditated – you just snapped..."

"I did..."

"On top of that – you just told me your husband wants a divorce..."

"Yes..."

"Oh yea – I can get you a deal..."

"Can you promise me a deal?"

"I won't lie – you might get more than 7 years – but you definitely won't get life in prison – not as long as I'm your attorney – I can promise you that..."

"Oh my God..." Jade whispered as she started crying... "Thank you!!"

"You're welcome – now let's talk about your husband..."

"Let's not..."

"Is your husband fucking Amber?"

"You don't pull any punches – do you?"

"I don't waste time..."

"I'm not sure..."

"Heart Tech is a million-dollar company..."

"You've done your homework..."

"Of course..."

"How does that help me?"

"I'll tell you how it helps us..."

"Us?"

"You let me represent you in your divorce..."

"Ooohhh..."

"Once you go to prison, your husband can't file for a divorce for two years..."

"Two years? Oh yes – this is perfect!" she laughed...

"You don't want to be married to him anymore..."

"That's not true..."

"Yes it is – understand?"

"Where are you going with this?"

"Well – your husband wants a divorce – you tell him you'll grant him an uncontested divorce – provided he buys you out and guarantees you alimony for every month you're in prison..."

"Oh shit – can I do that?"

"You can do that..."

"What's the catch?"

"Thirty three percent..."

"That's your fee? Thirty three percent?!"

"You're going to get a settlement of around $500 thousand – plus alimony of at least a thousand a month – when you get out of prison – you won't have to go down to welfare or go to a shelter..."

"What if I don't get that much?"

"You can sit in prison, drag this out in court – or you can sit in prison, put your settlement in an account, let it earn interest, and have at least a million when you get out – it's your call..." he answered as he got up to leave...

"Wait!!"

"Yes?"

"I'd be a damn fool if I let you walk out that door..."

"That's what I'm talking about!" he exclaimed as he sat back down, pulled out some papers, and had Jade sign them...

"Congratulations..." he said as he shook her hand...

"What happens now?" she asked as he put the papers in a folder, put the folder in his briefcase, and got up to leave...

"Now I go to work..." he answered as he left...

"Smalls!"

"Hello Beverly..." Smalls greeted as he walked into her office and sat down...

"What brings you here?"

"I represent Jade Heart..."

"You represent Jade Heart? Yea – okay..."

"I'm serious!"

"Why would you take a case you know you can't win?"

"I'm bringing you a gift..."

"Cut the shit – I can't stand your ass – and you can't stand mine!"

"That's true – but I still have a gift for you..."

"Okay – I'll bite – what do you have for me?"

"My client is willing to plead guilty to 2nd degree arson and 2nd degree attempted murder – no trial – 7 to 10..."

"Aaaa Haaa Haaa Haaa!! Aaaa Haaa Haaa Haaa Haaa!!

"Okay – you're amused..."

"You can't be serious!"

"I'm serious!"

"Smalls – it was nice seeing you..."

"So that's it? You'd rather go trial?"

"Yes!"

"Why?!"

"Because – I'll finally get a chance to beat you!"

"Yes you will – and you'll tie up the courts for months, you'll be exhausted at the end of the trial – you'll cost the taxpayers thousands of dollars – and I'll plead her out anyway..."

"At least she'll get more than 7 to 10!"

"You know what – you could just make me a counter-offer – I might be tempted to bring it back to my client – but if you'd rather go to trial..." he said as he got up to leave...

"12 years!"

"12 years – not 12 to 15 – not 12 to life – 12 years – and she's done?"

"Hurry up and take this to your client..." she laughed as she slipped Smalls some paperwork..."

"You Fuckin' Bitch!" Smalls laughed...

"Gotcha!"

"Aiight, Aiight – you got me!" Smalls laughed as he got up to leave...

"Excuse me?"

"Yes?"

"Aren't you forgetting something?"

"I was trying to..." he sighed...

"Bring it on in..." she commanded as she leaned forward and puckered her lips. Smalls grabbed her face in his hands, closed his eyes, kissed her hard, and then he pushed her back... "Thank you Baby!" she exclaimed...

"Shu the fuck up!" he laughed as he left her office...

"Jade Heart – please report to the visiting room..." the warden announced over the loud speaker...

"Thank God – it has to be my attorney – nobody else gives a damn!" she exclaimed as she hurried to the visiting room... "Smalls! Please tell me you have good news..."

"I have news..."

"Oh no – just tell me now – I'm not getting a deal – right?"

"Come with me..." he said as he waited for her to get up and then he took her by the hand and walked her to the attorney-client room...

"Please – I can't take it – just tell me!"

"Have a seat..."

"Okay – I'm sitting..." she sighed as she sat down. Smalls sat down with her and took out the paperwork...

"I got you a deal..."

"Oh my God! Thank you, thank you, thank you!" she squealed as she began kissing his face...

"Uh uh – I'm married!"

"Sorry – I can't help it – I'm so happy!"

"It's not as good as I thought it was going to be..."

"You said you were going to get me 7 to 10..."

"I said I'd try..."

"You promised me I wouldn't do life..."

"You won't..."

"Okay – thank God – I can breathe now – how much time do I have to do?"

"12 years..."

"12 years? What happened to 7 to 10?"

"I had to kiss the Bitch in the mouth to get 12 years!"

"Did you really kiss her in the mouth to get me a deal?"

"That's what I said..."

"Damn – you really work for your clients!" she laughed...

"So you'll take the deal?"

"12 years – it's a hell of a lot better than 20 – I'll take it..."

"Okay!" he exclaimed a she pulled the file out his brief case, took the papers out, and handed her a pen...

"Where do I sign?"

"Sign all the pages that have a red X..."

"Okay..." she sighed as she began signing the papers. Smalls sat there patiently as she signed them all and then he spoke...

"Now I take this back to the District Attorney, she schedules a court appearance, and you get sentenced..."

"I thought I didn't have to go to trial..."

"You're not going to trial – you're going to appear in front of a judge – I present your plea to the judge – the District Attorney tells the judge she's agreed to your plea – the judge will either sentence you or he may ask you to allocate – that means the judge will ask you to tell him what happened in your own words..."

"Won't he already know what happened?"

"Yes – but anytime a defendant pleads guilty without a trial and also agrees to more than a few years in prison, the judge wants the defendant to give an allocution to make sure the defendant understands what they're doing..."

"What if the judge doesn't accept my plea? What if he thinks I'm not getting enough time?"

"I don't see that happening..."

"But what if it does?"

"If the judge doesn't accept the plea deal – then you go to trial..."

"You kissed that Bitch in the mouth to get me a deal – he better not make me go to trial!"

"Exactly..." he said as he got up...

"Will you be there?"

"Absolutely..."

"How long will this take?"

"About 30 days..."

"Do I get time served?"

"Yes – every day you serve counts towards your sentence..."

"11 years... 11 months... and 25 days to go..." she sighed...

"I'll be in touch..." Smalls said as he gave her a hug...

"Thank you..."

"You're welcome..."

"Good morning!" Dr. Preston greeted as he came into my room...

"Good mooorrrnnning!" I sang...

"You're in a good mood – that's good – how are you feeling?"

"I'm feeling better than yesterday..."

"That's what I like to hear..."

"Am I going home today?"

"Yes – but I want to go over your test results..."

"Okay..."

"As you know, your EKG was normal – but your CT scan showed a couple of things..."

"Okay..."

"Your heart looks normal – but it looks like you have an infection in your chest – this could be due to all the smoke you inhaled during the fire...”

“Uh huh...”

“Are you asthmatic?”

“Yes...”

“Okay – I’m going to put you on steroids and penicillin for 10 days – finish all your medication – I’ve already scheduled a follow-up appointment for you to see me in two weeks – make sure you keep that appointment...”

“Yes doctor...”

“Okay – I’m going to sign these papers, I’m going to have you sign these papers, and then as soon as they discharge you - you can go home...”

“Thank you Dr. Preston...”

“Hey!” Chris exclaimed as she walked in...

“Hello – I’m Dr. Preston – are you here to take her home?”

“Can she go home?”

“Yes – It’ll take them about 2 hours to discharge her...”

“Why does it always take so long to discharge people?”

“Look – if it were up to me you could leave right now – but if anything happens to you before they discharge you – you’re responsible...”

“I’ll wait for them to discharge me Dr. Preston...” I sighed...

“Thank you – listen – I have other patients – I gotta run – I’ll see you in two weeks...” he said on his way out...

"He's nice..." Chris said...

"Yes he is..." I agreed...

"Look in the bag..." she said as she handed the bag to me...

"Oh wow! Hey Babies!" I exclaimed as I started playing with them...

"They really needed to be cleaned and saged...

"I know – especially after being in all that smoke..."

"They look brand new..."

"They do..."

"I have everything set up at your place..."

"Thank you Chris..."

"He has no idea what's coming..."

"Nope..."

"I thought you said you wanted to wait until he was divorced?"

"I did – but now that she's been arrested, she could get 15 to life – and she'll make him wait two years for spite..."

"Make him wait two years?"

"If your spouse goes to jail – you can't divorce them for 24 months – and then after you file, you have to wait another 90 days after you file..."

"How do you know this?"

"I looked it up..."

"Okay – I'm gonna stop by your place and put the crystals in the display case – do you want me to come back here and drop off your key?"

"Naaa – you can drop it off the next time I see you..."

"Are you gonna be able to get in?"

"Oh yea – I have an extra set of keys..."

"Okay – le'me get going before Sid gets here..."

"Thank you Chris..."

"You're welcome..." she said on her way out...

"Chris!" Sid exclaimed as he pulled her into a hug...

"Hi Sid!" she exclaimed...

"Did you see Amber?"

"I just did – listen – I gotta go – I'll see you later..." she said as she hurried off...

"Hmm – I guess she was in a hurry..." he shrugged...

"Good morning My Queen..." he said as he came into the room...

"Good morning My King..." I said as I jumped up out the bed...

"Come here..." he breathed as he pulled me close to him and kissed me hard...

"Wow – what was that for?"

"I saw what you did..."

"What'd I do?"

"You saved my crystals..."

"Yea... I did..."

"Why didn't you tell me?"

"I didn't want to..."

"Where are they?"

"They're safe..."

"Does Chris have them?"

"No..."

"Okay..." he sighed as he sat down...

"I'm going to get dressed..."

"You're being discharged?!"

"Yes..."

"When?!"

"As soon as they come tell me I can go home..." I answered as I closed the door and locked it..."

"You sure you wanna be alone in the room with me behind a closed door?"

"It'll just be a minute..." I answered as I got dressed in a hurry...

"Can I open the door now?"

"Yes..."

"Okay..." he said as he got up and opened the door just in time...

"Ms. Morrison – you've been discharged – here's a copy of your discharge papers – you can leave whenever you like..."

"Bye!" I exclaimed as I snatched my bag, grabbed Sid's hand, and pulled him out the room, down the hall, to the elevator...

"Did you see the doctor?" Sid asked...

"I saw the doctor – we'll talk later –let's go!"

"Okay, okay!" he laughed as the elevator door opened...

"Excuse us..." I laughed as we got in and a few others got off...

"I'm glad to see you're so happy..."

"I'm glad to be happy..." We didn't speak again until we got off the elevator...

"Where would you like to go?"

"Home..."

"That's nice – where's home?"

"Lafayette Blvd..."

"Oh that's right – you live downtown..." he said as we walked over to the car. Sid opened the door for me, I got in, he got in, and then we left the parking lot...

"We're here..."

"Oh wow – you can walk to work..."

"When I had a job I could..." I sighed as I got out the car...

"C'mon – show me where you live..." he said as he took my hand...

"Right this way..." I said as we started walking towards the entrance...

"Good morning Amber..."

"Good morning Charles – this is Obsidian, My King..."

"Good morning your majesty..." Charles said as he shook Sid's hand...

"Good morning Charles – please call me Sid...

"Nice to meet you Sid..."

"Y'all here about that fire down the street from here?"

"That was my building..." Sid answered...

"You own Heart Tech?"

"Yes..."

"Oh wow – how's the building?"

"They were able to keep the fire from spreading..."

"That's good – insurance companies don't like to pay out nothing – always giving you an excuse – but don't let me keep you..."

"I'll see you later Charles..." I said...

"Have a good day..." Charles said as we went inside towards the elevator...

"Is he always like that?" Sid laughed...

"Yes – he means well though..." I said as we got in the elevator. We didn't speak until we got in front of my door... "We're here..." I said as I took out my keys and opened the door... "C'mon in..."

"This is nice..." he said as he closed the door...

"Thank you..."

"You get lots of sunlight..."

"Yes I do – I love that..."

"You introduced me as your King..." he breathed as he pulled me into a kiss...

"You are My King..."

"And you are My Queen..." he breathed as he started pushing me back towards the couch...

"Sid... wait..."

"Okay..." he sighed as he sat down...

"I want us to talk..."

"Uh oh..."

"What happened yesterday?"

"You really want to talk about that?"

"Yes..."

"Sigh... When I got there, you were being put in the ambulance..."

"Right..."

"After you were taken by ambulance, we went down to the police station..."

"We?"

"Chief Johnson, me, and Jade..."

"Jade was there?"

"Yes – you don't remember?"

"I mean at the police station..."

"Yes..."

"So you made a report?"

"Jade was arrested..."

"Oh..."

"She's not getting out..."

"Can she make bail?"

"No – and even if she could – she doesn't have anywhere to go..."

"What about your place?"

"She could go to our place if she could make bail – but she's not making bail..."

"So after you had her arrested – you came to see me..."

"Yes..."

"How did it go with Mrs. Osgood?" I asked. I could tell Sid was happy I changed the subject...

"It was a little rough in the beginning..."

"Why?"

"I told them everything and Beautiee wants to put it in my book..."

"You don't want that in your book?"

"She wants to put what happened to you in the book..."

"Oh..."

"I told her I didn't want the video in my book, so she said she'd tell he readers I couldn't bear to watch my wife hurt My Queen..."

"Aww..."

"She also wants to put our readings in the book..."

"I really am a part of your story..."

"Yes – you are..."

"I can't wait to read it..."

"I signed a contract..."

"So it's official?"

"Yes..."

"Congratulations..."

"Thank you..." he breathed as he kissed me...

"I thought you were going to come back to the hospital..."

"I'm sorry – after I signed the contract they had a surprise party for me to welcome me to Beautiful Publications..."

"Oh wow! That's great!"

“They had hors d’oeuvres and a lot of champagne...”

“Come on – let me show you around...” I said as I got up...

“Lead the way...” he said as he got up...

“Well - as you know, this is the living room...”

“Yes... I know...”

“The Kitchen is over here...”

“Okay...”

“The bathroom is this way...” I said as I took his hand and pulled him towards the bathroom...

“It’s cute...” he laughed as I pulled him inside...

“C’mon...” I said as I pulled him out of the bathroom and pulled him into the bedroom...

“My crystals!”

“You said you saw what I did...”

“You save them from the fire...”

“Yes...”

“God I love you...” he breathed as he pulled me into a kiss...

“I love you too...”

“Let me make love to you... please...”

“I want to...”

“What’s stopping you?”

“I don’t want it to be the three of us...”

“It won’t be...”

“I don’t want to start something with you until you’re finished with her...”

"I'm finished with her..."

"Had she been to court yet?"

"I don't know..."

"That's what I mean..." I sighed...

"You want me to call and find out what's going on with her?"

"I want it to be over..."

"So do I..."

"Can you stay here with me?"

"Yes..." he answered as a phone started ringing...

"Is that your phone?"

"That's not my phone – I think it's your phone..." he answered as he took a new Samsung Galaxy 21 Ultra out his other pocket and handed it to me...

"For me?"

"Yes..."

"Thank you!" I exclaimed as I answered... "Hello?"

"How do you like your new phone?"

"Chris! When did you – you know what – never mind!" I laughed...

"I wanted to surprise you..." Sid said...

"I couldn't resist!" Chris laughed...

"Jade Heart report to the visiting room..." the warden said over the speaker...

"Thank God!" she exclaimed as she hurried to the visiting area...

"Good morning..." Smalls said...

"Good morning... Jade responded, even though she felt uneasy...

"Come with me..." Smalls said as he walked towards the attorney-client room. When they got to the room Jade spoke...

"What's wrong?"

"Come inside..." he said as he held the door open for her...

"Oh boy..." she sighed as she sat down...

"You go to court tomorrow..."

"That's good – right?"

"I need to tell you something..."

"What's wrong?"

"We have a deal in place for 12 years..."

"Yes – I know..."

"The District Attorney is okay with it..."

"Okay..."

"The judge we're going in front of is a hard-ass..."

"Oh no..."

"He might not take the deal..."

"Can he do that?"

"Yes – we talked about that..."

"So he wants me to do life in prison?"

"He may want 15..."

"Oh God – I can't!" Jade exclaimed as she started crying...

"Listen..." Smalls said as he wiped her eyes...

"Okay..."

"This isn't definite – he might accept the deal – I just had to let you know it was a possibility..."

"Okay... thanks for letting me know..."

"You're welcome..."

"What time is court?"

"9:30 – they'll wake you up around 4 am – they like to have the inmates in court early..." he answered as he got up to leave...

"See you tomorrow?"

"See you tomorrow..." he said as he left. When he got outside, he called Beverly right away...

"Yes Smalls?"

"It's done..."

"Was she crying?"

"Yea..."

"Good – she won't get that much sleep – she'll be a wreck and the judge will take pity on her – she's not confrontational – right?"

"No..."

"Okay - I'll see you tomorrow..."

"Thanks Beverly..."

"You're welcome Baby..."

"Shut the fuck up!" Smalls laughed as he hung up...

"This is Sid..."

"Mr. Heart?"

"Who's calling?"

"This is Attorney Smalls – I'm representing your wife..."

"What can I do for you?"

"Your wife is due in court tomorrow morning for sentencing..."

"What time?"

"9:30..."

"Do I need to be there?"

"You don't need to be there – but you might want to be..."

"Why?"

"Mr. Heart – I know you're angry – but after tomorrow, you might not see your wife again..."

"Why should I care about that?"

"Because you need closure..."

"I already have all the closure I need..."

"As I said – you wife's due in court for sentencing..."

"Sentencing? She's not going to trial?"

"She agreed to take a plea..."

"What does that mean?"

"It means she'll do 12 years instead of 15 to life..."

"12 Years?!"

"Yea..."

"For arson and attempted murder?"

"We thought it would be in everyone's best interest to avoid a trial..."

"So she gets off easy because Amber didn't die – wow!"

"Okay – that's enough..." I said as I went over to Sid, snatched the phone out his hand, and hung up..."

'Umm... you wanna give me back my phone?"

"Nope..." I answered as I put both phones in the kitchen drawer and went to sit down...

"You know I can go get my phone if I want it – right?"

"You could – but you won't..."

"You're pretty sure of yourself – aren't you?" he laughed...

"You said you were done – right?"

"Yes..."

"So why would you go get your phone when you could come get me?" I asked as I jumped up and ran into the bedroom...

"Uh uh – don't run now!" he laughed as he picked me up and threw me on the bed...

"Sid... wait..." I laughed...

"I'ma tell you like you told me..." he laughed as he tickled me – nope..."

"Stop..." I laughed... "My stomach hurts..." I laughed...

"Okay..." he laughed as he kissed me... I'll stop..."

"Sid..." I breathed as we continued kissing...

"Please... don't make me stop..."

"Sid... look..." Sid stopped kissing me and looked over at the display case. We both watched in awe and shock at what we saw...

"Oh my God... it's so beautiful..." he whispered as he started crying. I started crying too as we continued looking at the crystals, gemstones, and spheres. The display case had three shelves. The 1st and 2nd shelf had two bowls each and they were filled with crystals and gemstones, and the bottom shelf had spheres and a few rough pieces – and everything was spinning... "I've never seen anything like this..." Sid whispered...

"I need to record this..." I whispered as I reached in my nightstand drawer, took out my camera, and began recording. The crystals and gemstones were glowing and swirling around their bowls harmoniously and the spheres were glowing and spinning around the bottom shelf horizontally... "I want to feel their energy..." I whispered as I went over to the display case and unlocked the door. We both gasped as the crystals and gemstones came out the display case, rose up to the ceiling, and started spinning around the room... "Oh my God!" I whispered as I lay back on the bed and continued recording. Moments later, the spheres left the display case, rose up to the ceiling, and spun around in unison with the crystals and gemstones...

"No one will believe this..." Sid whispered...

"Yes... they will..." I whispered as I stopped recording and put the camera back on the night stand...

"I could watch this all night..." Sid sighed...

"They want us to make love..."

"So do I..." he breathed as he pulled me into a kiss. I pulled Sid down on top of me and when he put his tongue in my mouth, it felt as if his body melted into mine. I don't remember how he got my clothes off or his, but I remember feeling his hands caressing me and I remember feeling my hands caressing him. We continued kissing and tussling on the bed as the crystals, gemstones, and spheres swirled around us, and once he entered me we both began feeling and experiencing orgasmic energy and pleasure...

"Huh... Sid..."
"Uugh... Amber..."
"Huh... Sid..."
"Uugh... Amber..."
"Sid... Huh... Oh God... Sid..."
"Amber... Uugh... Oh God... Amber..."

The orgasmic energy and pleasure increased in intensity as it ran down our legs, into our feet, into our toes, back up our feet, back up our legs, up our torsos, down our arms, and down into our hands. Our fingers intertwined as our orgasmic energy and pleasure moved from our hands, up our arms, into our shoulders, across our necks, and into our throat chakras as we cried out of our eyes and our mouths simultaneously...

"My King... I'm cumming... I'm cumming..."
"I'm cumming with you My Queen... I'm cummuning with you..."
"Huh... Huh... Huh... Huh..."
"Uugh... Uugh... Uugh... Uugh..."
"Hhhuuuhhh!"
"Uuuggghhh!"

We continued crying and kissing as the orgasmic energy began to descend, and then I noticed what was happening with the crystals, gemstones, and spheres...

"Sid... look..." I picked up the camera again, hit record, and we watched as the spheres continued to spin as they began to drop down from the ceiling, go towards the display case, and realign themselves on the bottom shelf...

"No one's going to believe this..." he whispered...

"Yes... they will..." I whispered as the crystals, and gemstones began to drop down from the ceiling, go towards the display case, and go into each bowl until they were all back in place and then the door on the display case closed...

"Is that going to happen every time we make love?"

"I hope so..." I breathed as I dropped the camera and pulled Sid into a kiss...

"Good morning..." Sid breathed as he kissed me...

"Good morning..."

"I don't want to leave you..."

"You don't have to..."

"Jade has court..."

"So?" I asked as I propped myself up on my elbow...

"I think I should be there..." he sighed...

"I think My King should honor his promise he made to his Queen – especially after last night..." I said as I climbed on top of him, straddled him, and sat on his dick...

"Oh..." he moaned as he grabbed my hips and began thrusting himself up inside me... "I... think... you're... right..."

"Let's go Jade!" the guard yelled as she turned on that bright neon light. Jade almost forgot where she was until she opened her eyes… "Deputy Hein will be here to escort you to breakfast – I'll see you later," she said as she went over to another prisoner…

"Well good morning to you too… Bitch…" Jade thought to herself as she got up off the bed and went towards the door…

"Good morning Jade – I hope you got some sleep – let's get you some breakfast…" Deputy Warden Hein said as he took her by the arm and escorted her down the corridor and past the rec room. Jade wasn't sure what was going on but she didn't ask questions – she just allowed him to lead her into another room with other prisoners... "Wait here – I'll be right back…" he said as he left the room…

"Hey… What's going on?" Jade asked a woman sitting next to her.

"We're all going to court," she answered.

"Oh… okay…," Jade smiled.

"I hope you like fried bacon - this ain't a fuckin' restaurant so make due…" Deputy Warden Hein said as he placed a box of sandwiches and a box of coffees on the table…

"Oh my God – that smells so good!" Jade exclaimed as she took a sandwich and a cup of coffee…

"This is your first time huh?" the woman asked...

"Yea..." Jade answered as she started chewing...

"What's your name pretty?" she asked.

"Jade..."

"Well I'm Sherry – it's nice to meet you..." she said as she extended her hand...

"Nice meeting you too..." Jade said as she shook her hand and started drinking coffee...

"Jade – let's go – now!" Deputy Warden Hein ordered as he walked back into the room. Jade stood up immediately, waiting for him to escort her to wherever she was going next. He took her by my arm and escorted her to another room, pushed her inside, came into the room, and closed the door behind him... "Sit down!" he ordered as he pointed to one of the chairs. He sat down in the other chair before he continued... "Stay away from Sherry...

"Did I do something wrong?"

"Listen to me Jade – Mary's been in here for a long time – she gets cozy with newbies, gets them to trust her, then reports what she learns to the D.A. for perks and favors..."

"Okay..."

"Finish your coffee – you'll all be cuffed together when you leave here – you'll step up into the van – and you'll all sit together until we got to the court house – once we get to the court house you'll be escorted off the van and into the waiting room – once you get in the waiting room you'll be un-cuffed; however, when you're called you'll be re-cuffed with your hands in front of you and I'll escort you to the Bailiff. The Bailiff will sit you down at the table with your attorney and then your cuffs will come off.

"Okay…" she sighed…

"Listen to me Jade – and this is very important – I need you to behave yourself – no outbursts – no flailing arms and hands – and whatever you do – don't open your mouth unless instructed – you hear me?"

"Yea…"

"Okay – now let's go…" he said as he stood up, grabbed her arm, and escorted her back into the room with Mary and the others so they could get cuffed. When they got to the courthouse it was extremely chaotic – "This way! Hurry Up! Move!" They didn't give a damn that the inmates were cuffed together – they just wanted them outta the way… "Move it!" Deputy Warden Hein yelled as he pushed Jade into everyone else in front of her. When they got inside the waiting room he removed the cuffs before he spoke… "Sorry I was kinda rough – please don't take it personal – they're watching us all like a hawk – they have cameras and eyes everywhere..." he explained as he took the cuffs off... "Okay – Jade – you're up – stand up and extend your arms out in front of you..." He waited for Jade to do as instructed and then he cuffed her wrists before he continued... "I'm going to take you into the court room – the Bailiff will escort you to the table with your attorney – do you remember what we talked about?"

"Yea..."

"Okay then – let's go..." he said as he grabbed her by the arm and escorted her to the court room. Once inside, the Bailiff grabbed her by the arm and started to escort her to the table where Smalls was waiting for her with a smile, as well as the judge...

"All rise." Everyone stood up. "Department One of the Superior Court is now in session. Judge Dulberg presiding. Please be seated..."

"Good morning, ladies and gentlemen. Calling the case of the People of the State of Connecticut versus Jade Heart. Are both sides ready?"

"Ready for the People, Your Honor..." Beverly said.

"Ready for the Defense, Your Honor..." Smalls said.

"Very good – we'll start with your opening statements..."

District Attorney's Opening Statement

"Your Honor,

On Wednesday, March 17th, at approximately 10 a.m., the defendant, Jade Heart, was arrested and charged with 1st degree arson at Heart Tech, located downtown, in Bridgeport, Connecticut. The defendant was also charged with the attempted murder of Amber Morrison in the 1st degree..."

Attorney Smalls's Opening Statement

"Your Honor,

My client has agreed to plead guilty to arson in the 2nd degree and attempted murder in the 2nd degree in exchange for a reduced sentence of 12 years..."

"Has the district attorney accepted this plea?" Judge Dulberg asked...

"The District Attorney's office has accepted this plea..." Beverly acknowledged...

"Will the defendant please rise?" Jade stood up along with Smalls... "Mrs. Heart – do you have anything to say for yourself?"

"I love my husband..."

"You have a strange way of showing it..."

"Your Honor... please... let me explain..." she pleaded as she started crying...

"Please – go ahead..."

"Those crystals are my husband's legacy. They've been passed down through three generations. As much as I love him, I've never understood that and I could never get into them..."

"That's your explanation?!"

"Your Honor... please..." she pleaded as she continued crying..."

"I'm listening..."

"He hired Amber and I saw her playing with the crystals..."

"So your employee was into the crystals?'

"Yes..."

"Is that when it started?"

"Yes..."

"Go on..."

"My husband came home and he told me he couldn't stop thinking about her..."

"Wait a minute – your husband told you he couldn't stop thinking about this woman he just hired?"

"Yes..."

"I see..."

"He started to tell me he watched her, he was fascinated with her, and then he told me she felt energy from the crystals – and that's when I knew he was pulling away from me..." At this point, Beverly and Smalls could see the judge was feeling sorry for Jade and they smiled briefly as Jade continued... "When my husband told me he wanted a divorce, I was devastated - and when he refused to make love to me, I decided to re-watch the video of them having lunch... and... she... touched... his... hand... and... I'm sorry – I can't!" she cried...

"Smalls – give your client these tissues!" the judge snapped...

"Yes Your Honor..." Smalls said as he hurried to get the box of tissues and handed the box to Jade...

"Mrs. Heart – I know this is difficult – I'm sorry – but can you take me to the day of the fire?"

"I was hurt - I was angry - she stole my husband's heart - I fired her - I only wanted to burn the crystals – I told her not to come back – she came back – she said crystals – I just wanted my husband back – Oh God – I'M SORRY!" she screamed as she began crying uncontrollably...

"That's it – I've heard enough – I'm accepting the plea – Mrs. Heart – you're hereby sentenced to 12 years – you'll begin serving your sentence immediately starting from Wednesday, March 17th, 2021 and you'll be released on Friday, March 18th at approximately 9 a.m..." As the judge banged the gavel, Beverly and Smalls noticed tears in his eyes as he got up from the bench and returned to his chambers...

"I'm... glad... that's... over..." Jade sniffed as Smalls held her...

"So am I..."

"When... will... I... see... you... again?" she sniffed...

"You're going to see me as soon as I serve your husband with these divorce papers..." he answered as he smiled...

"Oh my God!" I forgot!" she exclaimed as she stopped crying and started smiling as the judge came out his chamber and returned to the bench..

"Attorney Smalls – I need to see you in my chambers..."

"Yes Your Honor..." Smalls acknowledged...

"Wait here – I'll be right back..." Smalls said. Jade sat down and waited...

"Is there a problem Your Honor?"

"Has her husband been served with divorce papers yet?"

"Not yet..."

"Hmm – does she have an attorney representing her in the divorce?"

"I'm representing her..." Smalls wondered what was going through the judge's mind as he started smiling...

"Is the divorce going to be contested?"

"No..."

"When you come back to file the papers, make sure it's on my calendar – and make sure you bring the defendant with you ..."

"May I ask why?"

"No you may not..." Judge Dulberg answered as he smiled and winked...

"Yes Sir..." Smalls acknowledged as he smiled...

"Sid..." I panted as I grabbed the bedspread in my hands and clenched my fingers – but he didn't hear me – he was somewhere else... "Sid..." I panted again. I was feeling orgasmic energy and pleasure, but I was also feeling something else – something more powerful – as he let go of my hips and grabbed my shoulders... "My King... Huh..."

"Yes My Queen... Yeesss..." he growled as he lay down on my back and breathed in my ear...

"Cum for your King..."

"Aagghh! Aagghh! Aagghh! Aagghh! Aaaggghhh!" Sid held my shoulders firmer, pounded faster, and came for his Queen...

"Uugghh! Uugghh! Uugghh! Uugghh! Uuuggghhh!" Sid lay back down on my back and I held us both up until my legs began to wobble and then we both collapsed on the bed... "My Queen..." he breathed in my ear and then he kissed me on the back of my neck and down my right shoulder...

"My King..." I breathed. I was unable to move and I didn't want to. Our orgasms were intense, the energy was intense, the power was intense – and in that moment, I knew exactly what Sid needed – and I was willing to give it to him...

"Well damn!" Chis exclaimed as she hung up...

"What's wrong?" Chandra asked...

"She's not answering the phone!"

"Well – what'd you expect?"

"Huh?"

"You cleaned their crystals, you saged them, you moved them into their new home – fully charged – ready to go to work once they were reunited with their owner – who just happens to be a King – a King that's finally been reunited with his Queen – why do you think she's not answering the phone?"

"They're fucking each other's brains out!" Christ exclaimed and then they both bust out laughing...

"This is Sid..."

"Good morning Sid – this is Beautiee..."

"How are you Beautiee?"

"I'm good – listen – I need to ask you something..."

"Okay..."

"Have you reconsidered putting the video in the book?"

"I'm not putting the video in the book – but I did watch the video – and I saw what Amber did – and I love her..."

"Okay – that's it – I need details – what time can you get in here to see me?" Beautiee laughed...

"I can stop by sometime this week – I need to go check on my building..."

"Okay – that's good – we can put that in the book too..."

"I have a lot more to tell you..."

"Could you ask Amber if she'd be willing to speak with me?"

"Sure – hold on a sec..." he answered and then he put the phone on mute... "Amber – would you be willing to speak to Beautiee?"

"About your book?"

"Yes..."

"Sure..."

"Okay – I'll tell her..." he said before he took the phone off mute... "Hey Beautiee – Amber said she'll speak with you..."

"Yes! Keep me posted!"

"Okay Beautiee – thanks for calling..."

"You're welcome – have a good day..."

"Thanks Beautiee – you too..." he said as he hung up...

"This is going to be a great book..." I said...

"Yea..." Sid sighed...

"What's wrong Sid?"

"I don't know..." I went over to him and took his hand...

"Come sit down..." We sat down on the couch and I took his hand again... "Talk to me..."

"Don't get me wrong – I'm happy Beautiee wants to publish my story – but at the same time – I feel like I'm celebrating Jade..."

"I get it..."

"You do?"

"Yes..."

"Thank God..."

"You want the book to be more about how we got reunited and less about how your marriage ended..."

"Yeesss!"

"I know how you feel – and I get that – but I also understand why Beautiee wants to include it in your book..."

"You do? Can you explain it to me then?"

"I'm a reader..."

"Okay..."

"As a reader, I want to understand how you go from zero to 100..."

"What?"

"You watch Criminal Minds – right?"

"Yes..."

"They always do a profile and they always give you an explanation as to why the criminal became a criminal..."

"That explains Jade..." he sighed...

"It explains you too..."

"I guess..."

"Think about it – some readers will start reading your book and think you just wanted out of your marriage without understanding what you went through – by including everything that led up to how we got together – especially the readings – it gives the reader insight – remember – I kept pushing you away – I talked to Chris because I needed to know and understand why I wanted you..."

"I told them that..."

"You did? What'd they say?"

"They cried..."

"Aww..."

"I think that's why Beautiee wants to talk to you..."

"I'm going to tell you something..."

"Okay..."

"I think you should go see Jade..."

"What?! Why?!"

"Because you need closure... and you need to forgive her..."

"Okay – where did My Queen go – and who am I talking to?!"

"Hear me out..."

"Okay – I'm listening..."

"You need closure and you need to forgive her for not accepting you and loving you for you..."

"If she really loved me..."

"She does love you..." I interrupted... "She loves you as much as she can – she just wasn't able to love you completely..."

"Can you forgive her?"

"When I was in the fire, I thought I was going to die – but after talking to Chris – I realized I wasn't going to die at all – and if I didn't go back there, your crystals wouldn't be here..."

"So you forgive her?"

"I'm not there yet – but as Chris Rock would say – I ain't sayin' it's right – but I understand..."

"Do you really want me to go see her?"

"I want you to do whatever you want..."

"Wait a minute – you just said you think I should go see her..."

"I do think you should go see her – but if you don't think you need to see her – then don't go see her..."

"How 'bout I just stay here with you for the rest of my life and forget about everything else?" he asked and then he pulled me into a kiss...

"I love you too – but you need to go see about your building – you'll need to speak with the insurance company, you'll need to speak with contractors, and you'll need an interior decorator – Heart Tech needs a facelift – you need to make it light, bright, and airy – and..."

"You're hired..." he breathed as he pulled me into his arms and kissed me hard...

"So..." I panted as I caught my breath... "I have my job back?"

"No – you've been promoted – you'll need to hire an office assistant to replace you..." he breathed as he kissed me again...

"Okay – go – I need to call Chris – I'll see you later..."

"I'll see you later..." he breathed as he kissed me again, and then he got up, took his phone out the drawer, and left...

"Oh so you finally took a break from the dick long enough to return my calls huh?"

"Shut the fuck up Chris!" I said and then we both bust out laughing...

"How are the crystals?"

"I don't know what you did to them – but oh my God!"

"All I did was clean them and sage them – same as I do my own crystals..."

"Oh so your crystals float and spin around the room when you and your wife make love too?"

"Okay – wait – what are you talking about?"

"I took Sid – well – I didn't take him – I made him chase me – and when he caught me, he picked me up and threw me on the bed...

"Aaa Haaa Haaa Haaa! He said c'mere woman!"

"The attorney for his wife called – they got into it – I snatched the phone from him, hung it up, and put our phones in the drawer – so he says you know I can go get my phone if I want it right – so I said why would you go get your phone when you can come get me – and then I ran into the room..."

"Oh shit – I know that's right!" she laughed...

"So when we caught me, he threw me on the bed and he started tickling me – my stomach was hurting from laughing so I told him to stop – so he stopped tickling me and started kissing me – and that's when I noticed the crystals, gemstones, and spheres..."

"What about them?"

"They were glowing – they rose up out their bowls – and they were spinning around their bowls..."

"Are you serious?!"

"Yes- and the spheres rose up and started spinning around the bottom of the display case..."

"Oh wow!"

"I wanted to feel their energy so I opened the display case – and that's when the crystals and gemstones floated up to the ceiling and spun around the room..."

"Oh my God – I wish I could've seen that!"

"I recorded it..."

"Yesses!! Send it to me!!"

"I'll send you both of them..."

"Both of them?!"

"So the crystals and gemstones floated up to the ceiling and started spinning around the room – and then the spheres left the bottom of the display case and floated up to the ceiling and spun around the room in unison with the crystals and gemstones..."

"They were feeding off the energy between you and Sid..."

"I told Sid they wanted us to make love..."

"Aww..."

"You said the crystals were feeding off our energy – I think we were feeding of theirs..."

"Really?"

"Chris – we had an all-night marathon – it was magical – and it was intense!"

"Damn!"

"And the crystals, gemstones, and spheres glowed and spun around the room until we were finished – and I recorded that too..."

"Oh God – I don't wanna see that!!" Chris laughed...

"Nooo – I recorded the crystals!!" I laughed...

"You recorded the crystals?!"

"After we finished making love, the crystals and gemstones came down from the ceiling and went back into their bowls in the display case – and then the spheres dropped down from the ceiling and went back into the display case – and then the doors closed…"

"Wooowww!!"

"Sid said nobody would believe it…"

"I believe it – I've seen psychic energy before…"

"Sid asked me if the crystals were going to do that every time we made love…"

"Maybe…"

"I'm not sure – I wasn't paying attention this morning – but I wouldn't've been able to see them from the position I was in anyway…"

"Oh shit – what position was that?"

"Face down – ass up!"

"Oh shit!!" she laughed…

"Last night I felt this energy – but this morning – I felt something different…"

"Different? I don't understand…"

"It was powerful – I've never felt anything like it – and when he reached his peak he lay down on my back and whispered in my ear – Cum For Your King…"

"Oh my God – I lose it whenever my wife starts talking shit in my ear!!"

"Girl – I fuckin' exploded!!"

"I see why you didn't answer my calls!!"

"Our phones were in the kitchen drawer…"

"So where's Sid now?"

"I told him to go check out his building – he's got some issues he needs to deal with…"

"Issues?"

"Well – he got a book deal with Beautiful Publications..."

"That's great!!"

"I think so to – but he wants the book to be more about us and less about her..."

"I can understand that..."

"I can too – but I told him she's part of how we got together so she needs to be in the story – and I told him he needs to go see her..."

"Why would you tell him to go see her?"

"He needs closure – and he needs to forgive her..."

"I agree he needs closure – but I don't know if he can forgive her for trying to kill you..."

"I told him he needs to forgive her for not living him completely because she did the best she could..."

"Damn – that was some good dick!!" Chris laughed...

"It wasn't his dick – it was you..."

"Me?"

"Yea – after I talked to you I realized I wasn't going to die – I was supposed to be there to save the crystals – and now they're here, they're energized, they're glowing, and they're happy..."

"They're happy alright – they're so happy they're floating..."

"Wait 'till you see the videos – it was beautiful..."

"I bet it was..."

"Beautiee wants to interview me for his book..."

"Are you gonna do it?"

"Oh yea..."

"Alright girl – le'me go – I've gotta feed Maui and then make dinner..."

"Alright Chris – I'll talk to you later..."

"We're closed!!" Sid yelled...

"Obsidian Heart?"

"Who is it?!"

"Attorney Smalls..."

"What can I do for you?"

"Can we talk?"

"Hang on..." Sid said as he opened the door...

"Thanks – can I come in?"

"We had a fire..."

"Yes – I know..."

"Oh – that's right – you were my wife's attorney..."

"I still am..."

"I don't understand..."

"Can we sit?"

"Come in my office..." Smalls followed Sid into his office and they both sat down...

"I'm representing your wife in her divorce..."

"HER DIVORCE??"

"You haven't served her yet – have you?"

"No..."

"Consider yourself served..." Smalls said as he placed some papers on Sid's desk..."

"ARE YOU SERIOUS?!" Sid exclaimed...

"Yes..."

"Okay – you served me – now get out..."

"You don't have a pre-nup..."

"So what?!"

"So my client is willing to give you an uncontested divorce – provided you buy her out and pay her $1,000 a month in alimony for as long as she's in prison..."

"WHAT?! BUY HER OUT?! PAY HER ALIMONY?! THIS IS MY COMPANY – I'M NOT BUYING HER OUTTA SHIT – FUCK HER – AND FUCK YOU TOO – GET THE FUCK OUT OF MY OFFICE!!"

"If that's what you really want..." Smalls sighed...

"That's what I really want!"

"Fine by me – I get paid by the hour..." he sighed as he got up to leave...

"What's that supposed to mean?"

"If you contest it – you'll be in court for years – you'll have to pay her a lot more than

$500k and $1,000 a month in alimony – your company's going to be worth more every year – she'll be entitled to a share of the profits, stock options – but I'll leave – you need time to think about it..." Smalls answered and then he got up, left Sid's office, went out into the lobby, and waited by the door...

"MUTHA FUCKAAAA!!" Sid growled...

"Yes... Yes I am!" Smalls laughed as he left the building...

"Who is it?" I asked as I went to the door...

"Sid..." I opened the door and when he came inside, I threw my arms around him...

"Hey My King..."

"Hey My Queen..." he breathed as he kissed me...

"What's wrong?"

"Nothing..." he sighed as he went to sit down...

"You need a drink?"

"Jade used to ask me that every day when I came home..." he answered as he started tearing up...

"Oh my God – Sid..." I whispered as I went to sit down next to him and took his hand... "What's wrong?"

"I'm sorry..."

"For what?"

"Smalls came by to see me..."

"Did Jade go to court?"

"He served me with divorce papers..."

"Jade filed for a divorce?"

"That's not all..."

"What else is there?"

"She's willing – that's a joke – she's willing to give me an uncontested divorce – provided I buy her out of Heart Tech – oh – I almost forgot – and she wants me to pay her alimony of $1,000 a month for the entire time she's in prison..."

"I thought Heart Tech was your company?"

"It is – but there's no pre-nup..."

"How much does she want?"

"$500k..."

"What?! Oh that's crazy!"

"Smalls said my company will be worth more every year – the longer it takes – the more she's entitled to..."

"Can you afford it?"

"I could if I take out a 2nd mortgage on Heart Tech..."

"What if you sell your house?"

"I'd be homeless..."

"You could always move in with your Queen..."

"Really?"

"Really..."

"I'll call Smalls tomorrow..."

"Tell him you're still thinking about it..."

"Why?"

"Take out a 2nd mortgage on Heart Tech – don't put your house up for sale until the divorce is final – once the divorce is final, you can put your house up for sale, pay off the 2nd mortgage, and move in with me..."

"God I love you..." he breathed as he kissed me..."

"I love you too – you want something to drink?"

"I don't want anything to drink..." he breathed as he pushed me down on the couch... "I want something to eat..." he breathed and then he went up under my skirt..."

"Oh wow – Sid – look!" I exclaimed as I sat up...

"Oh wow..." Sid whispered as we both watched the crystals, gemstones, and spheres circling above us...

"How'd they get out here?" he whispered...

"I didn't lock the display case..." I whispered. Sid began to pull my blouse up over my head and I didn't object. After he pulled my blouse over my head, he tossed it to the floor, he unhooked my bra, and tossed it to the floor...

"Stand up..." he commanded. I stood up and he pulled my skirt along with my panties down to the floor. I stepped out of them and Sid took my hand...

"Wait..." I whispered as I pushed his suit jacket off his shoulders. As it hit the floor, I ripped his shirt open and I the buttons fell to the floor as I pushed his shirt off his shoulders. I loosened his belt, unzipped his pants, and when I pushed his pants and boxers off his ass, his dick sprung to attention...

"I think they're waiting for us..." he whispered as I began to pull his t-shirt up. He lifted his arms and after I pulled it over his head, he pulled me into a kiss and we were tonguing each other down as our hands were all over each other... "Mmmph... Mmmph... Mmmph..."

"Hmmph... Hmmph... Hmmph..."

"Get on your back..." he commanded...

"Yes My King..." I panted as I got on my back and he dropped down on his knees, lifted my leg up, put it on his shoulder, and began eating... "Oh... Sid... Huh... Huh..." I don't know what it was about him but the orgasmic energy was high, it was intense, and I felt as if my soul was leaving my body as I arched my ass up off the couch and cried out... "Haah... Haah... Haah... Haah... Hhhaaahhh!!!" Sid didn't let up and when I looked up at the crystals, gemstones, and spheres, they were still circling above us and I was beginning to feel dizzy... "Sid... Stop..." I panted. Sid lifted his head and smiled at me, knowing that he defeated me, and I could tell that he was pleased with himself... "Look..." I whispered as I pointed up towards the ceiling and stood up...

"Wow... they're still circling..."

"Get on your back..." I commanded...

"Yes My Queen..." he breathed and then he got on his back. I got on the couch between his legs on my knees and when I bent down, his dick sprung up towards my mouth...

"Is this for me?" I asked and then I took his dick in my mouth and began swirling my tongue around it...

"Yessss..." he moaned as he grabbed both sides of my head and played in my hair... "It's... all... for... you... uuugghhh..." he moaned as he arched his ass up off the couch and pushed his dick in my mouth further. Rather than take control, I let him control the pace and enjoy my mouth and when his legs began to tremble, I steadied myself on his thighs... "Uugghh... Uugghh... Uugghh... Uugghh... Uuuggghhh!!!" Sid looked up at the crystals, gemstones, and spheres as I continued sucking his dick and just as I started getting dizzy, so did he... "Amber..."

"Hmmm?" I answered with his dick still in my mouth...

"C'mere..." he growled as he pulled me up on his chest, pulled me down, and kissed me hard... "I love you..." he whispered...

"I love you too..." I whispered back...

"Look..." he whispered as he pointed up towards the ceiling...

"Oh wow..." I whispered as we both watched the crystals, gemstones, and spheres go back towards the bedroom... "Do you think they'll come back out if we go for round two?" I breathed...

“Only one way to find out...” he breathed as he put me on my back, spread, my legs, and eased himself inside me as he pushed his tongue in my mouth...

"Good Morning..." Sid breathed in my ear...

"Good morning..." I yawned as Sid turned me on my back and got on top of me...

"Sid..."

"Yes My Queen..." he breathed a she kissed me...

"I need coffee..."

"My Queen..." he breathed as he spread my legs and eased himself inside me and began thrusting... "You... wouldn't... dare... deny... your... King... would... you?"

"Never... my... King..." I moaned...

"Jade Heart please report to the visiting area..." the warden said over the loud speaker...

"Who is it this time?" she sighed as she went to the visiting area and sat down. When she saw it was Smalls, she got excited... "Hey Smalls!"

"Good morning..." he said as he sat down...

"Should we go to the attorney/client room?"

"Sure..." They both got up, went to the room, and when Smalls closed the door, she got nervous...

"What's wrong?"

"Everything's going as planned..."

"It is?"

"Your husband was served yesterday..."

"Already?!"

"I told you – I don't like to waste time..."

"How'd it go?!"

"It went just as I expected..."

"Oh shit – he was pissed – wasn't he?!"

"Yes..."

"I knew it!!"

"That's a good thing..."

"Why is that a good thing?!"

"Because – before he threw me out, he let me get in his head..." Smalls answered as he smiled a sinister smile...

"You really are a mother fucker!!" Jade laughed...

"That's pretty much what he said..." Smalls laughed...

"How long should we wait?"

"We won't be waiting long..."

"Really?"

"He'll get back to me by the end of the week – maybe even sooner..."

"What if he wants to go to court?"

"The longer it takes - the more money we get..."

"I sure hope he takes the deal..."

"He will..."

"How do you know?"

"Because he's smart..."

"Huh?"

"When you first met me – what did you tell me?"

"I told you I'd be a damn fool to let you walk out that door..."

"And he'd be a damn fool not to take the deal..."

"So how much do you get out of this deal?"

"It's in your paperwork..."

"I don't have my paperwork..."

"Oh – that's right – I have it..."

"So... how much?"

"$165k..."

"Wow – I see why you kissed that Bitch in the mouth!!"

"She has nothing to do with this..."

"You never told her?!"

"Why would I?!"

"Mutha Fucka!!" Jade laughed...

"Yes..." Smalls laughed...

"So you get $165k – I get $335k..."

"You'll get more than that..."

"I will?"

"You're going to get $1,000 per month for 12 years..."

"That's right – that's $52k per year..."

"You put $100 on your books in here – the rest you put in your account – that's $46,800 per year – you add that to $335k – you'll add an additional $561,600 to your account – you'll have over a million by the time they add interest..."

"Wow!!"

"You have to be disciplined though – I've seen prisoners do stupid shit – get high – dress to impress – gamble – help out other prisoners – make new friends – don't do any of that shit – I don't care how tempted you are!!"

"I won't – don't worry..."

"Good – I need to go now – I'll keep in touch..."

"Thank you Smalls..."

"You're welcome..." he said as he left...

"I'll never get used to this..." I sighed as we lay in bed looking up at the crystals, gemstones, and spheres...

"I love watching them..."

"Me too..."

"I'll get your coffee now..." he said as he got up out the bed...

"I'm coming with you..."

"I know – I heard you..." he laughed as I followed him into the kitchen and the crystals, gemstones, and spheres went back into the display case...

"Can we go to Queen's Delight?"

"Sure – you still want coffee?"

"Yes..."

"Okay – I'll make us some coffee – and we'll talk..."

"Where are your other employees?"

"They're located throughout Fairfield County..."

"How many locations do you have?"

"I have Bridgeport, South Norwalk, Stamford, Stratford, and Milford..."

"Wow – you have 5 buildings?"

"No – I have one building and 4 offices..."

"I was wondering why I never saw anyone in the building but you and me..."

"I have the offices because it's easier to send my reps out from different locations – if I sent everyone out from Bridgeport, it'd take longer for the reps to service my clients..." he explained as he handed me a cup of coffee...

"Ooohhh.... this is good..."

"I'll make a note of it..."

"What else can you make?"

"Whatever you want - I can make drinks..."

"Oh nice..."

"And I can make food..." he laughed...

"What kind of food?"

"Whatever you want to eat..."

"Right now I'm in the mood for shrimp and grits..."

"Once I move in with you, I'll do the shopping – and then I'll be able to cook whatever you want..."

"I like the sound of that..."

"Since you're hungry, we need to get in the shower..."

"Okay – go 'head..."

"Excuse me?"

"Yes My King?"

"Aren't you coming?"

"If I come in the shower with you, we'll end up starving..." Sid came over to me, took me by the hand, led me into the bathroom, and closed the door... "What the hell is that noise?" I asked as I turned to look at the door. Sid opened the door and we both bust out laughing as the crystals, gemstones, and spheres made their way into the bathroom and started glowing and circling around the ceiling...

"Welcome to Queens Delight – what can I get you?" the hostess asked...

"I'll have shrimp & grits..." I answered...

"Make that two..." Sid answered...

"Would you like anything to drink?"

"Coffee..." we both answered...

"I'll be right back..." the hostess said as she went to place our order. After she came back with the coffee, I spoke...

"What are we doing after breakfast?"

"We're going to Bank of America – I need to speak to Marlowe about the mortgage..."

"Is Marlowe a mortgage specialist?"

"He's the President..."

"Oh wow..."

"Bazil introduced me to him – he's a nice guy – he'll help make the process faster..."

"That's good – the sooner we can be done with this – the better..."

"I couldn't agree more..."

"Here's your food – if you need anything else – please let me know..." the hostess said as she placed our food on the table...

"Could you give us two steak, egg, and cheese sandwiches to go?" I asked...

"I sure can..." the hostess said as she went to place our order...

"You really are starving..." Sid laughed...

"I'm good right now – but this won't hold me all day..."

"I can't wait until I can hold you all day..." he said as he licked his lips and smiled mischievously..."

"Here's your order to go – and your check..." the hostess said as she put both on the table...

"Thanks..." Sid said a she put cash in the bill holder... "Keep the change..."

"Thank you sir..." she said as she went to help the next customer..."

"Are you ready?" Sid asked...

"Yes... I'm ready..." I answered as I smiled mischievously...

"Now see – you're lucky we're going to the Bank..." he laughed as we got up to leave...

"Sid – Good morning – how are you?" the gentleman asked a she came over to us...

"I'm fine Marlowe – this is Amber..."

"Nice to meet you Amber – I'm Marlowe..."

"Nice meeting you too..."

"Marlowe – I need your help..." Sid said...

"Come with me..." Marlowe said as we followed him to his office... "Umm – Sid..."

"Oh it's okay – Amber is my Office Assistant – you can speak in front of her..."

"Okay – I'm sorry to hear about the fire..."

"Thanks..."

"Was there a lot of damage?"

"No – thank God..."

"That's good – how can I help you?"

"I'm here to apply for a 2nd mortgage on my building..."

"Your insurance company isn't taking care of the damages?"

"They are – this is personal..."

"I don't think that's a good idea..."

"Oh... I see..."

"I think it's better for you to get a business equity loan – you'll get the money faster..."

"I like the sound of that..."

"How much are you looking for?"

"$500k..."

"Hmm – you've been doing business with us for 10 years – your credit's not an issue – we can have that deposited into your account by the end of the week..."

"As in Friday?"

"I think so – I have all your information – I can fill it in and print you out an application – we'll check a few details – once corporate approves it – you'll get the money..."

"Thank you Marlowe..."

"You're welcome – let me print this out for you – you can sign it before you leave – if all goes well – which I'm pretty sure it will – I'll be calling you in a couple of days..." Marlowe explained as he got up and went to the printer...

"He's really nice..." I said...

"Yes he is..." Sid agreed...

"Here you go – sign every page that has a stickie – and I'll call you in a couple of days..."

"Thanks Marlowe..." Sid said as he began signing the application... "Done!"

"Okay!" Marlowe laughed as he picked up the papers...

"Thanks again..." Sid said...

"You're welcome..." Marlowe said as we left...

"Let's go see Bazil and Beautiee..." Sid suggested...

"Where are they located?"

"They're in Milford..."

"Okay..." I sighed...

"You wanna go get the car or take the train?"

"Let's go get the car..."

"Okay – c'mon..." he said as he took my hand and we walked down the street...

"Sid?"

"Yes My Queen?"

"I don't want to tell them about the crystals..."

"They already know about them..."

"I mean I don't want to tell them about what they do when we make love..."

"Didn't you tell Chris?"

"Yes – but she won't tell the world..."

"What if Beautiee wants to interview her?"

"Chris won't do that – she's okay with being in the book – but that's it..."

"Okay – we're here..." he said as he opened the door for me to get in...

"Thank you My King..." I said as I got in the car...

"You're welcome My Queen..." he said as he closed the door and went to get in on the other side...

"I'm not ready to sell my house..." he sighed...

"Why not?"

"Because I'm not ready to deal with going through Jade's things – I don't even know what to do with them..."

"I can go to the house with you..."

"You sure?"

"Yes..."

"You'll help me pack up the house?"

"No – we'll hire a company to pack the house for you – we'll just be there to supervise – you can put her things in storage or throw them out..."

"Thank you..." he sighed as he took my hand and kissed it...

"You're welcome..."

"I don't know what I'd do without you..."

"You won't ever have to worry about that..." I said as we rode the rest of the way...

"Sid – this is a surprise!" Bazil said as we walked in...

"Hi Bazil – this is Amber, My Queen..."

"Nice to meet you Amber..." Bazil said as he shook my hand...

"Nice to meet you too..."

"Come with me..." We followed Bazil down to his office and when we went inside, Beautiee was there...

"Sid! Thanks for coming in!" she exclaimed...

"Beautiee – this is Amber, My Queen..."

"Hi Amber!" she exclaimed as she got up and pulled me into a hug...

"Hi Beautiee..." I laughed...

"Can we get you anything?" Bazil asked...

"We have some sandwiches in the car..." I answered...

"We have a cafeteria – you can get whatever you like..." Bazil said as he got up...

"Okay..." Sid said as we followed Bazil and Beautiee to the cafeteria...

"Oh... this is nice!" I exclaimed...

"Get whatever you want..." Beautiee said...

"I'll get an Italian club..."

"I'll get a roast beef..." Sid said...

"You want everything on those?" the cook asked...

"Yes sir!" Sid exclaimed...

"Coming right up!" the cook acknowledged...

"What are you drinking?" Bazil asked...

"Water..." Sid laughed...

"Seriously?"

"For now..." Sid answered...

"Amber – I can't wait to speak to you..." Beautiee said...

"Sandwiches are ready!" the cook announced...

"C'mon – we'll let the men get it..." Beautiee said as she took my hand and led me out the cafeteria...

"I can't believe you work here..."

"I can't believe it myself..."

"Really?"

"Oh yea – when Bazil met me – I was in a bad place – he saved my life – and I didn't know it at the time – but I save his life too..."

"Wow..."

"You don't have to be nervous..."

"Am I that obvious?"

"Yea..." Beautiee laughed...

"I can't help it – Sid is introducing me as his Queen and you were at his wedding with Jade...

"I'm in no position to judge anybody..."

"Really?"

"Amber – my husband cheated on me with his best friend – and I got arrested for trying to kill my husband, killing his best friend, and killing our female lover..."

"Oh my God!"

"You haven't read any of my books – have you?"

"No..."

"Before you leave – I'm going to give you copies of In The Arms Of A Gangster..."

"Ohh... I like that title..."

"That's my story..." she said as she took me into the conference room and closed the door...

"Umm... why are we in here?"

"I wanted you all to myself..."

"Umm..."

"Amber – relax – I won't bite you – unless you want me to!" Beautiee laughed...

"Can I have my sandwich?"

"Sure – I'll be right back..." Beautiee answered as she went to get my sandwich...

"How's Amber?" Sid asked...

"Nervous as hell!" Beautiee laughed as she picked up my sandwich, a bottle of water, and came back into the conference room...

"How's it going with you and Amber?" Bazil asked...

"She's amazing..." Sid sighed...

"That's great..."

"This is the most pussy I've gotten in a long time..."

"Are you serious?"

"I'm serious..."

"You and Jade..."

"We had sex a couple of times a week – but I always felt like Jade was sexing me because she felt it was an obligation..."

"I don't understand..."

"Amber wants me – the real me – she's turned on by me – she submits to me..."

"Yea – that's like me and Beautiee..."

"So you know what I'm talking about..."

"Oh yea – we had to sound-proof our bedroom!" Bazil laughed...

"Who makes more noise?"

"It depends on the day and the position!" Bazil said and then they both bust out laughing...

"I had Amber face-down, ass up the other day..."

"I have Beautiee face-down, ass up almost every day!" Bazil laughed...

"I'm in love with Amber..."

"I get it..."

"You do?"

"I fell in love with Beautiee overnight..."

"Thanks..."

"For what?"

"For not judging me..."

"I'm the last person to judge anybody..." Bazil laughed...

"Okay Amber – here you go..." Beautiee said as she gave me the sandwich and the water...

"Thank you..."

"Do you mind if I record this?"

"I guess not..."

"If I ask you anything you don't want to answer – just tell me you're not answering that..."

"Okay..." I sighed as I took a bite of the sandwich...

"So – when did you first meet Sid?"

"About two weeks ago..."

"Did you know he was married at that time?"

"Yes – I knew he was married when I went for the interview..."

"Oh – so you applied for a job?"

"Yes..."

"How long did you work there?"

"About a week and a half..."

"Up until you got fired?"

"Yes..."

"Tell me about the crystals..."

"I've always been into crystals – when I saw them I started playing with them..."

"What do they do?"

"It depends on what you need – crystals affect everyone differently – for example – you, Bazil, and your employees should be wearing shungite..."

"Why?"

"Shungite absorbs the energy that comes off electronics..."

"Interesting..."

"You can get it in a pendant that's shaped like a triangle – you can wear it around your neck or you can hang it near your computer..."

"You think that will help my employees?"

"Crystals don't do anything for anyone that doesn't believe crystals are nothing more than rocks..."

"Oh – like Jade..."

"Yes..."

"How are you so sure that crystals are more than rocks?"

"Go in any store – pick up a crystal you're drawn to – you'll feel the energy..."

"Hmm – that's interesting..."

"Have you ever gone to a spa?"

"Of course..."

"They use essential oils, they use hot rocks, and they use crystals to make the atmosphere peaceful, tranquil, and calming..."

"That's true..."

"People accept that without question – but you tell someone you collect crystals or gemstones – they want to tell you they're nothing but a bunch or rocks or they want to tell you you're crazy..."

"Has anyone ever told you you're crazy?"

"That and a few other things – but I'm just like my grandmother – and she collected crystals too..."

"I can see why Sid's drawn to you..."

"I'm drawn to him too..."

"I was told you had a reading to help you understand why you were so drawn to Sid..."

"Yes..."

"Can I print a copy of that reading in the book?"

"That's up to Sid..."

"Okay – I'm done – is there anything you want to add?"

"No..."

"Okay – thanks for coming in..." Beautiee said as she reached for her recorder and turned it off... "C'mon – let's get you back to Sid..."

"Okay..." I agreed as I got up and we went back to their office...

"Hey My Queen – how'd it go?"

"It went fine..." I sighed. Beautiee went over to her desk and hit the intercom...

"Joselyn?"

"Yes Beautiee?"

"Could you bring a copy of In The Arms Of A Gangster in here please?"

"Yes Beautiee..."

"Thank you..." I waited for Joselyn to come in the office... "Joselyn – this is Amber, Sid's Queen..."

"Pleased to meet you your highness..."

"Nice to meet you too – please call me Amber..."

"Can I ask you a personal question?"

"Sure..."

"Are you really a Queen?"

"According to a reading we both had done with Phoenix Cards – in a past life, Sid was a King, I was his Queen, and our lives' ended tragically..."

"Phoenix Cards? Like Tarot Cards?"

"Yes – the difference is that Phoenix Cards tell you about your past lives..."

"Oookkaayy..." Joselyn said as she handed the books to Beautiee...

"I'll sign these for you – and then they're all yours..." Beautiee said...

"Thank you Beautiee..."

"You're welcome Amber..."

"Bye – it was nice meeting you..." Joselyn said as she left their office...

When she got to her own office, she started shaking her head back and forth...

"What's wrong?" Sam asked...

"Babe – I just met Amber..."

"She's the one that's going to be in Sid's book?"

"Yes – she's his Queen..."

"His Queen?"

"I said nice to meet you your highness – I thought she really was a Queen!" she laughed...

"So she's not?"

"She says they had a reading done with Phoenix Cards – and according to the reading – Sid was a King, she was his Queen, and their lives ended tragically..."

"If they like it – I love it – but the real Queen is right here..." Sam said as he pulled Joselyn into a kiss...

"Thank you King..." she said as she kissed him back...

"I'm glad we went to speak to them..." I sighed as we got in the car...

"Me too..."

"I told Beautiee about the crystals..."

"I thought you said you weren't going to do that?"

"I told her all about how I played with your crystals – and then I reminded her that people go to the spa all the time and no one questions their use of essential oils, hot rocks, or crystals – but as soon as you tell somebody you collect crystals – they want to tell you you're crazy!"

"Have I told you I love you?"

"Yes you have..."

"I bet she won't ask you anything else..." Sid laughed...

"I also told her she should order shungite pendants for her, Bazil, and their employees..."

"What's shungite?"

"Shungite absorbs the energy from electronics – you should wear it around your neck or hang it near your computer..."

"When you go back to work, I want you to order shungite pendants for all the employees..."

"Yes My King..." I said as I pulled him into a kiss...

"This is Judge Dulberg..."

"Your Honor – this is Attorney Smalls..."

"Smalls! What can I do for you?"

"My Client needs to be released for 24 hours..."

"Which client would that be?"

"Jade Heart..."

"You need to have a very good reason or there has to be extenuating circumstances..."

"I do Your Honor..."

"I'm listening..."

"Her husband was served yesterday..."

"Ah yes – the divorce..."

"Yes Your Honor – my client just wants to pack up her things before her husband goes through them and decides what happens to them..."

"That's not really considered extenuating circumstances..." he sighed...

"Thank you Your Honor – I'll let my client know..."

"Smalls – wait!"

"Yes Your Honor?"

"Fax the request over – I'll sign it..."

"Thank you Your Honor..." Smalls said as he hung up...

"Valarie?"

"Yes Smalls?"

"Fax it over!"

"He said yes?!"

"He said yes!!"

"This is Deputy Warden Hein..."

"This is Attorney Smalls..."

"Yes Smalls..." he sighed...

"My client, Jade Heart, has been granted a 24-hour release..."

"Is that right?"

"Yes... that's right..."

"How'd you get the judge to agree to that?"

"I asked..."

"Fax me the paperwork..." he sighed...

"I'm so glad to be home!" I exclaimed...

"I'm glad to be home too..." Sid breathed as he began to kiss me on my neck...

"Sid..."

"Yes My Queen..."

"I'm... hungry..."

"Mmmm... so am I..." he breathed as he pulled me into a kiss..."

"I... want... the... sandwiches..."

"You're pregnant..." he sighed...

"I'm not pregnant – I'm just hungry..." I laughed...

"Okay..." he laughed... "We'll heat up the sandwiches. I went to sit down on the couch and kicked my shoes off... "Here..."

"Thank you..." Sid sat down next to me and we started eating....

"Oh my God – this is sooo good!"

"I can't believe you're this hungry!" he laughed...

"You're eating right along with me!" I laughed...

"Point taken..."

"So – when should we go over to your house?"

"I was thinking maybe I should go by myself..."

"Really? Why?"

"I've been thinking about what you said..."

"Okay..."

"You're right..."

"About what?"

"I need closure..."

"So you really want to go by yourself?"

"I want to go by myself tomorrow – after tomorrow, you can come with me...

"Okay..." I sighed...

"Guard?"

"Yes Jade?" Gertrude answered...

"I need to go to the infirmary..."

"Are you having a medical emergency?"

"I've been nauseous and I'm having diarrhea..."

"Fine – I'll take you to the infirmary..." Gertrude sighed as she opened the cell...

"You've been nauseous?" the nurse asked...

"Yes..."

"Diarrhea?"

"Yes..."

"How long has this been going on?"

"About a week..."

"I'll give you a quick exam – we'll draw some blood – and we'll see what's going on..." the nurse said as she began to examine Jade... "Your eyes look good..."

"Thank you..."

"Your ears are clear..."

"That's good..."

"Your glands aren't swollen..."

"That's good..."

"Open wide..."

"Aaahhh...."

"Your throat's irritated – but that's because you've been throwing up – how's your appetite?"

"I'm hungry all the time – I think I just eat because I'm bored..."

"Is there any chance you're pregnant?"

"Pregnant?"

"You do have a husband – right?"

"Oh my God..."

"When was your last period?"

"I haven't had my period in a couple of months..."

"I'm going to take some blood..." the nurse said as she prepared the tubes...

"I can't have a baby in prison..."

"Jade – relax – let's see what's going on before you start stressing yourself out..."

"Too late..." Jade sighed...

"Jade Heart please report to the visiting room..." the warden said over the loud speaker...

"Smalls must have news..." Jade sighed as she went to the visiting room. When she got there, Smalls was waiting for her...

"Smalls!"

"Good morning..."

"Do you have news?"

"I have a surprise for you..."

"He signed the papers!"

"Not yet..."

"What then?"

"I spoke to Judge Dulberg..."

"Uh Oh..."

"I asked him to let you out for 24 hours..."

"Oh my God!" she squealed as she started jumping up and down... "Thank you, thank you, thank you!"

"You're welcome – but I need you to listen to me..."

"Okay!" she squealed...

"I convinced the judge to let you out for 24 hours to give you a chance to clear your things out of the house..."

"Oh my God – thank you!" she whispered as she started to cry...

"You'll have an ankle monitor placed on you – you'll be transported from here to your house – the clock starts from the time they pick you up – you have 24 hours to pack up whatever you can – they will be back to pick you up the next morning – you go in there – you pack up as much as you can – and please – this is important – don't leave the house – don't check the mail – don't open the door – stay in the house – pack up your things – and be ready before they come – when they get there they won't wait for you – understand?"

"I understand... but..."

"But what?"

"I don't have any boxes or packing tape..."

"I stopped at U-Haul and picked up a few things for you..."

"Thank you!"

"You're welcome..."

"How will I get my things out of the house?"

"Sign this..." he said as he put a piece of paper in front of her...

"What's this?"

"It says you give me permission to act on your behalf – read it..."

"I don't have to read it – I trust you..." she said as she started reading the paper... "Okay – I'll sign it..."

"Good..." Smalls said as he handed her a pen...

"Thank you so much!"

"You're welcome – I'll see you tomorrow..."

"Wake up..." Gert said as she banged on the cell...

"What time is it?"

"Time for you to get up..." Gert answered as she opened the cell...

"Why so early?"

"You want me to tell them you wanna go back to sleep or you want me to tell them you're ready to be released?"

"Oh shit – never mind – I'm up!" Jade exclaimed as she jumped up...

"Sit down – I need to put this ankle monitor on you..." Jade sat down, Gert put the ankle monitor on her, and then she took Jade by the arm...

"I'll go – you don't have to pull me..." Jade laughed...

"It's not personal – it's just procedure..." Gert explained as she led Jade down to the infirmary...

"Why am I here?"

"Good morning Jade..." the nurse said...

"Good morning – am I here for more bloodwork?"

"That won't be necessary..."

"Oh God – am I sick?"

"Jade – you're not sick – you're pregnant..."

"Oh my God – I can't have a baby in prison – what am I going to do?!" she cried...

"Jade..." the nurse said as she touched Jade's hand... "You don't have to make a decision right now – you're going to be released today – go home – being outside this facility might give you some clarity..."

"Okay..." she sniffed...

"C'mon – they don't like to be kept waiting..." Gert said...

"I'm coming..." Jade said as she hopped down off the table...

"Smalls!" Jade exclaimed as she ran towards him and threw her arms around him...

"Jade – you're shaking – what's wrong?"

"Let's go!" the officer snapped as he yanked Jade away from Smalls and snapped the cuffs on her...

"Was that necessary?" Smalls snapped...

"Look – I've got a back-log – I don't have time to cater to your clients!"

"Aiight – I gotchu..." As soon as Smalls said it, a chill went up the officer's spine...

"I'm sorry – I didn't mean to do that – I just need to hurry up..."

"I'm not the one you owe an apology to..."

"I'm sorry Mrs. Heart – it won't happen again – let's get you in the car so we can get you home – we're on both on the clock..." he said as he opened the door. Smalls followed behind them...

"I'll be back here tomorrow morning at 9 a.m. sharp – please be outside..."

"She'll be outside..." Smalls said...

"Here..." Smalls said as he handed her the key...

"I can't believe I'm home..." she whispered as she started to cry..."

"Come on – let's go inside..." When they got inside, Jade broke down...

"I don't know what I'm going to do!" she cried...

"You're going to pack your things..."

"I don't give a damn about these things!"

"Jade – what's going on?"

"I'm pregnant!"

"Listen to me..." Smalls said as he took her face in his hands and wiped her eyes... "You're going to be okay..."

"No I'm not – my husband doesn't want me – I'm going back to prison – I can't carry a baby and have them snatch it away from me!"

"Jade..."

"No Smalls – No!"

"Do you trust me?"

"I guess..."

"Have I steered you wrong yet?"

"No..." she sniffed...

"So you trust me – right?"

"Yes... but..."

"You trust me – right?"

"Yes..."

"Tell your husband you're pregnant..."

"Why? He doesn't want me..."

"It's not about you – it's about the baby..."

"But..."

"You trust me – right?"

"Yes..."

"Okay then – now that we have that settled – I'm leaving..."

"You're leaving?"

"You want me to stay?"

"I'd love for you to stay – but I need to do this by myself..." she sighed...

"Yes you do..."

"Thank you Smalls..."

"You're welcome..." he said and then he left...

"Oh shit – I can take a shower alone!" Jade exclaimed as she hurried upstairs...

"Where are you going?" I yawned...

"I'm going to stop by the house right quick – I haven't checked my mail..." he answered as he bent down to kiss me...

"Why didn't you wake me up?"

"You looked so peaceful..."

"Hurry back My King..."

"I will..." he breathed as he kissed me. I got sad and started tearing up when I heard the door close...

"What the hell is wrong with me?" I asked as I got up, put on my robe, and went into the kitchen...

"Damn – it's a good thing I came over here – this mailbox is full!" Sid exclaimed as he took the mail out the box... "I might as well go inside and sort through this..." he said as he unlocked the door... "I can't believe I'm back here..." he sighed as he put the mail on the table in the foyer...

"Smalls – is that you?"

"Oh hell no!!" Sid whispered as he hurried upstairs. When he got to his bedroom, he heard the water running so he went towards the master bathroom... "Jade..." he whispered as his body began to betray him. Sid's dick got hard and he reached down to rub it as he continued watching her...

"How long are you going to stand there watching me before you come in here and fuck me?" she asked as she turned to face him. Sid took one look at her body, stripped out of his clothes, stepped in the shower, and grabbed Jade around her waist... "Oh Sid..." she breathed as she threw her arms around him. Sid pushed her back against the wall, lifted her leg up, and thrust himself up inside her... "Oh Sid... Yes... Fuck me... Just like that..."

"Ugh! Ugh! Ugh!"

"Don't stop... Yes... Fuck..."

"Ugh! Ugh! Ugh!"

"I'm cumming... I'm cumming... Huh... Huh... Huh..."

"Ugh! Ugh! Ugh! Ugh! UUGGHH!!"

"Sid..." she breathed as he picked her up and she wrapped her legs around him. Sid carried her to the bed, threw her down on her back, and picked up where he left off... "Oh Sid... Yes... Fuck me..."

"Ugh! Ugh! Ugh!"

"God I missed this dick... Yes... Give it to me..."

"Ugh! Ugh! Ugh!"

"Sid... Huh... Fuck... I'm cumming again... Huh... Huh... Huh... HHHUUUHHH!!"

"Ugh! Ugh! Ugh! Ugh! UUGGHH!!" Sid collapsed on Jade and they both lay still for a few moments...

"You've never fucked me like that before..." she breathed as she kissed him. Sid pushed his tongue in her mouth and tonged her down as his dick started getting hard again...

"Hmmph... Hmmph... Hmmph..."

"Mmmph... Mmmph... Mmmph..."

"Hmmph... Hmmph... Hmmph..."

"Mmmph... Mmmph... Mmmph...

"HMMPH... HMMPH... HMMPH... HMMPH... HHMMMMMPPHH!!"

"MMMPH... MMMPH... MMMPH... MMMPH... MMMMPPPPHH!! Sid..."

"Yes Jade..." he breathed as he kissed her..."

"I'm pregnant..."

"I'm sorry – this was a mistake..." he said as he got up..."

"A MISTAKE?!" she creamed as she jumped up off the bed... "I TELL YOU I'M PREGNANT AND YOU TELL ME IT'S A MISTAKE?! HOW DARE YOU!!" she screamed as she slapped him. Sid stood there seething. His eyes turned to slits. He wanted to hit her but he knew better...

"I wasn't referring to the baby – I was talking about us..."

"Us?! So you fucked me for nothing?!"

"I'm sorry Jade – when I saw you in the shower – I got caught up in the moment – you asked me to fuck you – I lost it..."

"So you still want a divorce?"

"Yes..."

"What about the baby? You expect me to have your baby in prison?"

"You won't have my baby in prison..."

"So you'll fight for the baby – but you won't fight for us?"

"I'm in love with Amber..."

"Yea okay – you just fucked the shit outta me – but you love Amber..."

"I do..."

"Did you ever love me Sid?"

"Yes..."

"Can't you learn to love me again?"

"I don't need to learn to love you – I never stopped loving you – but after what you did – we can't go back..."

"We can go forward – we can raise our child – we can start over..."

"We might've been able to do that before I met Amber – but now that I've found My Queen – I can't let her go..."

"Your Queen?! Mutha fucka – I'm your Queen – I'm your wife – and I'm pregnant!!"

"I signed the divorce papers..." he lied...

"I'll tell Smalls I've changed my mind – I'm having your baby – fuck Amber – you're mine!!"

"I suppose I can't stop you if that's what you really want to do – I'll raise my child as long as you're in prison – but I still want a divorce – no matter how long it takes – now that I've met

Amber – our marriage is over...” he sighed as he started getting dressed...

“Unfuckin’ believable!! How’s your precious Amber going to feel when you tell her I’m pregnant?! How’s your precious Amber going to feel when you tell her you fucked me – and by the way – if you don’t tell her – I will!!”

“Thank you Jade...”

“Thank you?! For what?!”

“For giving me the closure I needed...” he said as he started to leave...

“So that’s it?! You fuck the shit outta me – I tell you I’m pregnant – and you’re leaving?!”

“There’s no reason for me to stay...”

“I just gave you a reason!!”

“Yes – you’re pregnant – but you haven’t shown one ounce of remorse for what you did...”

“Sid – please – wait – we can start over – we can put this behind us...”

“What about what you did to Amber?!”

“I told her not to come back – why couldn’t she just stay away – all I wanted was you – she never should’ve come back – we could’ve changed the locks – it’s all her fault!!” Jade cried...

“Good bye Jade...” Sid said as he left the bedroom. When he got downstairs, he picked up the mail, put it in his briefcase, opened the door, went outside, and broke down crying on the stoop...

"Hey My King – oh my God – what's wrong?!" I asked as I started tearing up...

"Please... don't hate me..." he cried...

"Come sit down..." As soon as we sat on the couch he grabbed me and cried on my shoulder...

"Sid... please... tell me..." I whispered as I cried...

"My Queen – I've failed you – I'm begging you for your forgiveness..." he cried as he dropped down on his knees...

"You saw Amber..."

"Yes..."

"You had sex with her..."

"Yes... I'm sorry..."

"This is why I said I didn't want to start anything with you until you were done with her – because I knew you weren't done with her..." I said as I tried to get up but Sid pulled me back down...

"Please My Queen! I'm begging you! Don't give up on me!" he cried...

"I'm not giving up on you..."

"Oh my God – I love you so much – I don't deserve you..."

"That might be true..." I sighed...

"Let me explain – please..."

"It doesn't matter – I knew this was going to happen – I should've waited – I didn't – and now look what happened – I brought this on myself..."

"No!! You are not to blame!! Let me explain – please..."

"Okay – explain..." I sighed as I rolled my eyes...

"I went to check the mail. I unlocked the door to go in the house. I was planning on sitting down, going through the mail, getting a few things, and leaving – but then I heard Jade..."

"Jade? She got out..."

"Yes..."

"I knew this shit was going to happen!!"

"Please – let me finish..."

"Go 'head!!"

"She called Smalls name – I thought she was upstairs waiting for him so I went upstairs to confront her... she was in the shower... I started watching her..."

"So you fucked her?"

"She asked me to..."

"Oh that's just great – aren't you a real fuckin' gentleman – you know what – get the fuck off me!!"

"No!! I don't want her – you're My Queen – I want you!!"

"Did you realize that before or after you fucked her?!"

"I just got caught up in the moment – I didn't know she was going to be there – I'm sorry!!"

"I'm sorry too..." I whispered as I started crying...

"Please... tell me you forgive me..."

"I forgive you..."

"I'll make it up to you – it'll never happen again – I swear..."

"Don't make promises you can't keep..."

"I have something to tell you..."

"Oh God – what now?"

"She's pregnant..."

"OH MY GOD!!" I screamed...

"I'M SORRY!! I DIDN'T KNOW!!"

"GET OUT!!"

"Please – I told her it's over – I still want a divorce – I want to be with you – please don't make me leave!!"

"Sid..." I whispered calmly..."

"Yes My Queen?"

"I need you to get up... and I need you to get the fuck outta here..."

"Okay – I'll go..." he said as he got up, he left, and I cried for hours...

"Thanks for meeting me..." Sid sighed...

"What the hell happened?!" Bazil exclaimed...

"I fucked up..." Sid whispered as he started crying...

"What happened?!"

"Jade happened..." Sid sighed. "I went to my house to check the mail. I went inside and I heard Jade call Smalls..."

"Oh shit – Smalls is fucking Jade?!"

"I ran upstairs – she was in the shower – my dick got hard – she caught me watching her – and then she said how long are you going to stand there watching me before you come in here and fuck me..."

"Oh Sid..."

"I couldn't help it – it was so good – after we got out the shower I threw her down on the bed and fucked her again - she started telling me she missed my dick and begged me to give it to her – I couldn't turn that down – and then she started kissing me and telling me I never fucked her like that before – my dick was hard again so I fucked her again..."

"Oh Sid..."

"I was thinking it was good – it was mutual – and that would be the end of it – but then she tells me she's pregnant – so I told her it was a mistake..."

"Sid!!"

"I wasn't talking about the baby – I was talking about me and her..."

"Oh..."

"She didn't like that shit one bit – she started screaming at me and slapped the shit outta me..."

"Can you blame her?!"

"No – but I told her I was in love with Amber, she was My Queen, and I wanted to be with her – Jade wasn't trying to hear that..."

"Beautiee would be devastated if I told her I didn't want to be with her after I got her pregnant..."

"Whose side are you on?!"

"I'm on your side – but you fucked up..."

"I know, I know – she said she wanted to start over and put all this behind us but I told her now that I've met Amber our marriage is over..."

"Oh damn..."

"Bazil – she tried to kill Amber – remember?!"

"I understand that – but..."

"She asked me if I ever loved her and if I could learn to love her again – I told her I didn't need to learn to love her again because I never stopped loving her – but she hasn't shown any remorse for what she did – she said what happened to Amber was her own fault because she should've stayed away and let us change the locks – after she told me that, I thanked her for giving me the closure I needed and I left..."

"She's still your wife – I know you don't want to be with her – but once you fucked her, you made her think you still wanted her..."

"I know – that was a mistake – but I still want a divorce – I know she's pregnant – I'll be there for my child – but I want to be with Amber – and now Amber doesn't want to be with me..." he sighed as he started tearing up...

"Listen to me..."

"Okay..."

"My wife left me..."

"What?! When?!"

"I cheated on her with my best friend – and she left me for a week..."

"You cheated on your wife?"

"Yes..."

"With your best friend?"

"Yes..."

"So..."

"Yes Sid – I was fucking a man – that's not the point!"

"What is the point then?"

"My wife was with Sonia for a week – and then she came back to me..."

"You cheated on your wife – with a man – and your wife forgave you – wow!!"

"Exactly..."

"I guess if your wife can forgive you – My Queen can forgive me..."

"She already has..."

"What makes you so sure?"

"She can't help it – she loves you..."

"That's true – but my wife's pregnant..."

"She got pregnant before you met Amber..."

"What if Amber can't accept my child?"

"If she can't accept your child, then she isn't really your Queen..."

"Amber!! Oh my God!! What happened?!" Chris exclaimed...

"He slept with her!!"

"Jade?!"

"Yes!!"

"She got out?!"

"Yea..."

"How?!"

"I don't care..."

"You don't care?!"

"I knew this was going to happen..."

"You did?!"

"I told him he needed to go see her – I knew he needed closure..."

"Okay – when you say you knew he needed closure – did you mean he needed to have sex with her?!"

"Nooo..." I cried...

"Exactly..."

"He begged me to let him explain..."

"What's to explain?!"

"He said he went over there to check the mail – he went in the house – she asked if it was Smalls..."

"Wait – wait – wait..." Chris interrupted... "He went to his house – she was in his house – and she was calling her attorney?"

"That's what he said..."

"So – if he thought she was having sex with her attorney..."

"How'd he end up fucking her?" I interrupted...

"Basically – yea..."

"He went upstairs – she was in the shower – she saw him standing there – she asked him to fuck her – so he did..."

"Well gee – he's such a fuckin' gentleman!!" she snapped sarcastically...

"That's exactly what I said!!"

"So did you break up with him?"

"No – but I told him to get the fuck out after he told me she was pregnant..." I sighed...

"Wwwhhhaaattt?!"

"She's pregnant... and I think I'm pregnant too..." I said as I started crying again...

"Oh Amber!"

"Well – you said I'm a unicorn – I've always live a magical life because I always allowed magic in – how's this for magic?!"

"Oh my God – I don't know what to say – I can't even imagine!!"

"I still want him..."

"I know..."

"He says he doesn't want her – I'm his Queen – he wants me..."

"He does..."

"I asked him if he realized that before he fucked his wife or after..."

"Oh my God – what did he say?"

"He said after..."

"I swear to God – he better fix this – he's really pissed me off!!"

"You?! Oh no – he's definitely in trouble now..."

"Are you going to take him back though?"

"Yes..."

"You really love him?"

"Yes..."

"Are you having his baby?"

"Oh yea..."

"I don't know if I could do it – he's going to go back and forth between the two of you – how are you going to deal with that?"

"I haven't thought that far ahead – I need to go to the doctor and find out if I'm pregnant before I do anything else..."

"She's going to be in prison for 12 years – they won't let her keep her baby – he'll probably want custody of his child..."

"I know..." I sighed...

"Do you have somewhere to go?" Bazil asked...

"I can't go back to the house..." Sid sighed...

"Why don't you get a room at the Holiday Inn?"

"I can't – that's too close to Amber..."

"Stay out here for the night – you can call Amber in the morning..."

"I need to talk to her..."

"Do you want her back?"

"Yeesss!!"

"Then you need to leave her alone..."

"How'd you do it?"

"I went online and checked my credit cards..."

"Huh?"

"Beautiee used my credit cards so I always knew where she was and what she was up to..."

"Damn – I wish I had that luxury..."

"Have you signed the divorce papers yet?"

"No – why?"

"Sign the papers..."

"I don't have the money to pay her yet..."

"How much do you need?"

"$500k..."

"Have you applied for financing?"

"Yes..."

"Did you see Marlowe?"

"Yes – be he said it may take a week..."

"I'll give you a loan..."

"Bazil – I can't let you do that..."

"You don't have a choice – now that she's pregnant – you need to sign those papers and get those papers filed before she bankrupts you..."

"You're right..."

"Go see Smalls – sign those papers – then tell him to call me..."

"Thank you Bazil..."

"You're welcome..."

"How may I help you?" Valarie asked...

"I'm here to see Smalls..."

"Do you have an appointment?"

"No..."

"May I have your name?"

"Obsidian Heart..."

"Are you here to sign your divorce papers?"

"Yes – how'd you know?"

"It's my job to know – you can sign them right now if you like..." she said as she pulled them out of a locked cabinet...

"Is Smalls here?"

"He's out – but I can take care of it – unless you'd rather wait for him..."

"I'll do it now – I have the papers in my briefcase..."

"Could you sign them both?"

"Both?"

"Yes – your copy and mine – this way I can get them filed with the court today..."

"Sure – I can do that..."

"This is Smalls..."

"Smalls – I don't want a divorce!"

"What?! Why?!"

"I told that mutha fucka I was pregnant – he tells me he wants to be with his Queen – he's going to take custody of my child after I give birth..."

"Wait – I'm confused – when did you speak to him?"

"He was here earlier..."

"He was at the house?"

"Yes..."

"Did you sleep with him?"

"Yes..."

"You slept with him – you told him you were pregnant – you told him you wanted to start over – and he rejected you – right?"

"Yea..."

"Jade – I'm sorry – I know that hurt – but I'm advising you to go through with the divorce..."

"Why?!"

"You'll be better off in the long run..."

"How am I better off?! I'll be pregnant and alone!!"

"You won't be alone..."

"What makes you so sure?!"

"I thought you trusted me?"

"Okay..." she sighed...

"Listen – I gotta run – sit tight – you'll get through this – okay?"

"Okay Smalls..."

"How may I help you?" Shireen asked...

"Hi Shireen – do you have any rooms available?" Sid asked...

"Yes we do..."

"May I have one?"

"How many nights will you be staying?"

"Two nights..."

"Okay – I have a king suite available – would you like that?"

"I'd like that..." he said a she gave Shireen his card...

"You're all set – you're in room 315 – here's your key..."

"Thank you..." Sid said as he took the key. Sid went to the elevator, got off on the 3rd floor, and went to room 315. After he was settled, he stretched out on the bed and, against Bazil's advice; he sent me a text...

"Hey My Queen,

I know I messed up, and I'm sorry. I signed the divorce papers earlier today and they'll be filed by the end of the week. I'm staying at the Holiday Inn in Milford, Room 315 tonight and tomorrow. If I don't hear back from you, I understand. Please know you'll always be My Queen no matter what you decide.

Love,
Your King"

"I love you too..." I whispered as I cried...

"Get up!"

"Huh?"

"Get up!"

"Is there somebody at the door?" I asked as I got up, opened the door, and looked out in the hallway... "Hmm – I must be hearing things..." I said as I shrugged my shoulders and closed the door...

"Go get a pregnancy test..."

"I know what I'll do – I'm going to go to the store and get a pregnancy test!" I exclaimed as I grabbed my purse, put on my shoes, and hurried downstairs...

"I hope they have Clear Blue..." I sighed as I went into the pharmacy. I already knew where the tests were, so I hurried over to that aisle and picked up two pregnancy tests, hurried back to the counter, went to the self-checkout, and hurried back home...

"Whew – you must know I gotta pee!" I exclaimed as I danced around to keep from peeing on myself as I opened the package. I got down on the toilet, put the test under me, and let it out... "Wooeee!" I exclaimed. I pulled the test out from under me and looked at the results... "Oh my God..." I whispered as I cried... "I'm pregnant..." I was so busy staring at the pregnancy test I didn't notice the crystals, gemstones, and spheres glowing and circling above me...

"Hey..." Beautiee said as she threw her arms around Bazil and kissed him fully...

"Beautiee..."

"Yes my Thirst Quencher?" she breathed...

"We need to talk – where are the kids?"

"They're upstairs..."

"Great – come with me..." he said as he took her hand and led her into the library... "Beautiee... wait..."

"No..." she laughed as she pushed him down on the couch and opened her robe... "I've been waiting for you..." she whispered as she grabbed her breasts and then she slowly moved her hands down to her pussy and spread her lips...

"Bring her to me..." Bazil commanded. Beautiee went over to him, stood up on the couch, and straddled his face...

"Oh God... Yes... My Thirst Quencher... Yeesss!" she moaned. Bazil grabbed her ass, held her down on his face, and fucked her pussy with his tongue... "Oh God Bazil... Fuck... I'm cumming... I'm cumming..."

"Feed meee!!" he growled...

"Haah... Haah... Haah... Haah... Haaahhhh!!" Bazil continued licking, sucking, and slurping until her orgasms subsided...

"Better?"

"Oh my God – Yes my Thirst Quencher... Yes..." she panted...

"Are you thirsty?"

"Yes my Thirst Quencher..." she breathed as she stepped down off the couch, put a pillow on the floor, dropped down on her knees, and opened Bazil's legs... "Oohh... You're happy to see me..." she breathed...

"Yeesss..." he breathed. Beautiee loosened his belt and then she used her teeth to unzip his zipper... "Oh shit – Okay!!" he exclaimed. Beautiee slid her tongue inside his boxers and began licking his dick... "Stop teasing me and let me fuck your mouth!!" he growled...

"I'll let you fuck my mouth when I'm ready..." she laughed as she put her mouth back on his boxers. Bazil grew impatient but his dick had a mind of its own and when the head peaked out his boxers, Beautiee swallowed his dick so fast it startled him...

"Fuck!!" he moaned as he grabbed both sides of her head and pushed his dick in further... "Yes Beautiee... That's it... Let me fuck your mouth... Uggh!!"

"Yes my Thirst Quencher..." she breathed and then she took him back in her mouth again down to his balls. Bazil was determined and frenzied whenever she submitted to him and this made him fuck her mouth harder...

"Oh fuck!! Yes!! Suck my dick!!" Beautiee relaxed her jaw and let some saliva drip down and Bazil lost it... "Beautiee... Fuck... I'm cumming!! I'm cumming!! Uuuggghhh!!" Beautiee swallowed every drop and continued sucking softly for a few moments... "C'mere!!" he growled as he pulled her up into a kiss and kissed her hard...

"I love you too..." she breathed... "What did you need to talk about?"

"I'll tell you later..." he said as he began rubbing his dick on her clit...

"Oh Bazil... Put it in... Please..."

"Please what?!"

"Please... my Thirst Quencher..." That was music to Bazil's ears as he thrust himself up inside her... "Oh God Bazil... Yes... Fuck me!!"

"Who am I?!" he growled in her ear as he grabbed her ass...

"My Thirst Quencher!!" she moaned...

"Damn right!!" he growled as she continued riding his dick...

www.ingramcontent.com/pod-product-compliance
Lightning Source LLC
LaVergne TN
LVHW050627100826
845148LV00011B/1761

* 9 7 8 1 7 3 5 6 6 2 0 7 7 *